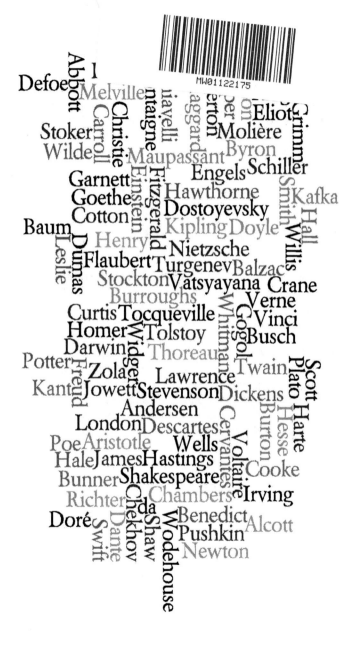

tredition®

tredition was established in 2006 by Sandra Latusseck and Soenke Schulz. Based in Hamburg, Germany, tredition offers publishing solutions to authors and publishing houses, combined with world-wide distribution of printed and digital book content. tredition is uniquely positioned to enable authors and publishing houses to create books on their own terms and without conventional manufacturing risks.

For more information please visit: www.tredition.com

TREDITION CLASSICS

This book is part of the TREDITION CLASSICS series. The creators of this series are united by passion for literature and driven by the intention of making all public domain books available in printed format again - worldwide. Most TREDITION CLASSICS titles have been out of print and off the bookstore shelves for decades. At tredition we believe that a great book never goes out of style and that its value is eternal. Several mostly non-profit literature projects provide content to tredition. To support their good work, tredition donates a portion of the proceeds from each sold copy. As a reader of a TREDITION CLASSICS book, you support our mission to save many of the amazing works of world literature from oblivion. See all available books at www.tredition.com.

 Project Gutenberg

The content for this book has been graciously provided by Project Gutenberg. Project Gutenberg is a non-profit organization founded by Michael Hart in 1971 at the University of Illinois. The mission of Project Gutenberg is simple: To encourage the creation and distribution of eBooks. Project Gutenberg is the first and largest collection of public domain eBooks.

The Feast at Solhoug

Henrik Ibsen

Imprint

This book is part of TREDITION CLASSICS

Author: Henrik Ibsen
Cover design: Buchgut, Berlin – Germany

Publisher: tredition GmbH, Hamburg - Germany
ISBN: 978-3-8424-8693-5

www.tredition.com
www.tredition.de

THE FEAST AT SOLHOUG.

by

HENRIK IBSEN

Translation by William Archer and Mary Morrison

INTRODUCTION*

Exactly a year after the production of *Lady Inger of Ostrat* — that is to say on the "Foundation Day" of the Bergen Theatre, January 2, 1866 — *The Feast at Solhoug* was produced. The poet himself has written its history in full in the Preface to the second edition. The only comment that need be made upon his rejoinder to his critics has been made, with perfect fairness as it seems to me, by George Brandes in the following passage:** "No one who is unacquainted with the Scandinavian languages can fully understand the charm that the style and melody of the old ballads exercise upon the Scandinavian mind. The beautiful ballads and songs of *Des Knaben Wunderhorn* have perhaps had a similar power over German minds; but, as far as I am aware, no German poet has has ever succeeded in inventing a metre suitable for dramatic purposes, which yet retained the mediaeval ballad's sonorous swing and rich aroma. The explanation of the powerful impression produced in its day by Henrik Hertz's *Svend Dyring's House* is to be found in the fact that in it, for the first time, the problem was solved of how to fashion a metre akin to that of the heroic ballads, a metre possessing as great mobility as the verse of the *Niebelungenlied*, along with a dramatic value not inferior to that of the pentameter. Henrik Ibsen, it is true, has justly pointed out that, as regards the mutual relations of the principal characters, *Svend Dyring's House* owes more to Kleist's *Kathchen von Heubronn* than *The Feast at Solhoug* owes to *Svend Dyring's House*. But the fact remains that the versified parts of the dialogue of both *The Feast at Solhoug* and *Olaf Liliekrans* are written in that imitation of the tone and style of the heroic ballad, of which Hertz was the happily-inspired originator. There seems to me to be no depreciation whatever of Ibsen in the assertion of Hertz's right to rank as his model. Even the greatest must have learnt from some one."

But while the influence of Danish lyrical romanticism is apparent in the style of the play, the structure, as it seems to me, shows no less clearly that influence of the French plot-manipulators which we found so unmistakably at work in *Lady Inger*. Despite its lyrical dialogue, *The Feast at Solhoug* has that crispiness of dramatic action which marks the French plays of the period. It may indeed be called Scribe's *Bataille de Dames* writ tragic. Here, as in the *Bataille de Dames* (one of the earliest plays produced under Ibsen's supervision), we have the rivalry of an older and a younger woman for the love of a man who is proscribed on an unjust accusation, and pursued by the emissaries of the royal power. One might even, though this would be forcing the point, find an analogy in the fact that the elder woman (in both plays a strong and determined character) has in Scribe's comedy a cowardly suitor, while in Ibsen's tragedy, or melodrama, she has a cowardly husband. In every other respect the plays are as dissimilar as possible; yet it seems to me far from unlikely that an unconscious reminiscence of the *Bataille de Dames* may have contributed to the shaping of *The Feast at Solhoug* in Ibsen's mind. But more significant than any resemblance of theme is the similarity of Ibsen's whole method to that of the French school — the way, for instance, in which misunderstandings are kept up through a careful avoidance of the use of proper names, and the way in which a cup of poison, prepared for one person, comes into the hands of another person, is, as a matter of fact, drunk by no one but occasions the acutest agony to the would-be poisoner. All this ingenious dovetailing of incidents and working-up of misunderstandings, Ibsen unquestionably learned from the French. The French language, indeed, is the only one which has a word — *quiproquo* — to indicate the class of misunderstanding which, from *Lady Inger* down to the *League of Youth*, Ibsen employed without scruple.

Ibsen's first visit to the home of his future wife took place after the production of *The Feast at Solhoug*. It seems doubtful whether this was actually his first meeting with her; but at any rate we can scarcely suppose that he knew her during the previous summer, when he was writing his play. It is a curious coincidence, then, that he should have found in Susanna Thoresen and her sister Marie very much the same contrast of characters which had occupied him in his first dramatic effort, *Catilina*, and which had formed the main subject of the play he had just produced. It is less wonderful that the same contrast should so often recur in his later works, even down to *John Gabriel Borkman*. Ibsen was greatly attached to his gentle and retiring sister-in-law, who died unmarried in 1874.

The Feast at Solhoug has been translated by Miss Morison and myself, only because no one else could be found to undertake the task. We have done our best; but neither of us lays claim to any great metrical skill, and the light movement of Ibsen's verse is often, if not always, rendered in a sadly halting fashion. It is, however, impossible to exaggerate the irregularity of the verse in the original, or its defiance of strict metrical law. The normal line is one of four accents: but when this is said, it is almost impossible to arrive at any further generalisation. There is a certain lilting melody in many passages, and the whole play has not unfairly been said to possess the charm of a northern summer night, in which the glimmer of twilight gives place only to the gleam of morning. But in the main (though much better than its successor, *Olaf Liliekrans*) it is the weakest thing that Ibsen admitted into the canon of his works. He wrote it in 1870 as "a study which I now disown"; and had he continued in that frame of mind, the world would scarcely have quarrelled with his judgment. At worst, then, my collaborator and I cannot be accused of marring a masterpiece; but for which assurance we should probably have shrunk from the attempt.

W. A.

*Copyright, 1907, by Charles Scribner's Sons. **Ibsen and Bjornson*.
London, Heinmann, 1899, p.88

THE FEAST AT SOLHOUG (1856)

THE AUTHOR'S PREFACE TO THE SECOND EDITION

PREFACE

I wrote *The Feast at Solhoug* in Bergen in the summer of 1855 — that is to say, about twenty-eight years ago.

The play was acted for the first time on January 2, 1856, also at Bergen, as a gala performance on the anniversary of the foundation of the Norwegian Stage.

As I was then stage-manager of the Bergen Theatre, it was I myself who conducted the rehearsals of my play. It received an excellent, a remarkably sympathetic interpretation. Acted with pleasure and enthusiasm, it was received in the same spirit. The "Bergen emotionalism," which is said to have decided the result of the latest elections in those parts, ran high that evening in the crowded theatre. The performance ended with repeated calls for the author and for the actors. Later in the evening I was serenaded by the orchestra, accompanied by a great part of the audience. I almost think that I went so far as to make some kind of speech from my window; certain I am that I felt extremely happy.

A couple of months later, *The Feast of Solhoug* was played in Christiania. There also it was received by the public with much approbation, and the day after the first performance Bjornson wrote a friendly, youthfully ardent article on it in the *Morgenblad*. It was not a notice or criticism proper, but rather a free, fanciful improvisation on the play and the performance.

On this, however, followed the real criticism, written by the real critics.

How did a man in the Christiania of those days—by which I mean the years between 1850 and 1860, or thereabouts—become a real literary, and in particular dramatic, critic?

As a rule, the process was as follows: After some preparatory exercises in the columns of the *Samfundsblad*, and after the play, the future critic betook himself to Johan Dahl's bookshop and ordered from Copenhagen a copy of J. L. Heiberg's *Prose Works*, among which was to be found—so he had heard it said—an essay entitled *On the Vaudeville*. This essay was in due course read, ruminated on, and possibly to a certain extent understood. From Heiberg's writings the young man, moreover, learned of a controversy which that author had carried on in his day with Professor Oehlenschlager and with the Soro poet, Hauch. And he was simultaneously made aware that J. L. Baggesen (the author of *Letters from the Dead*) had at a still earlier period made a similar attack on the great author who wrote both *Axel and Valborg* and *Hakon Jarl*.

A quantity of other information useful to a critic was to be extracted from these writings. From them one learned, for instance, that taste obliged a good critic to be scandalised by a hiatus. Did the young critical Jeronimuses of Christiania encounter such a monstrosity in any new verse, they were as certain as their prototype in Holberg to shout their "Hoity-toity! the world will not last till Easter!"

The origin of another peculiar characteristic of the criticism then prevalent in the Norwegian capital was long a puzzle to me. Every time a new author published a book or had a little play acted, our critics were in the habit of flying into an ungovernable passion and behaving as if the publication of the book or the performance of the play were a mortal insult to themselves and the newspapers in which they wrote. As already remarked, I puzzled long over this peculiarity. At last I got to the bottom of the matter. Whilst reading the Danish *Monthly Journal of Literature* I was struck by the fact that old State-Councillor Molbech was invariably seized with a fit of rage when a young author published a book or had a play acted in Copenhagen.

Thus, or in a manner closely resembling this, had the tribunal qualified itself, which now, in the daily press, summoned *The Feast at Solhoug* to the bar of criticism in Christiania. It was principally composed of young men who, as regards criticism, lived upon loans from various quarters. Their critical thought had long ago been thought and expressed by others; their opinions had long ere now been formulated elsewhere. Their aesthetic principles were borrowed; their critical method was borrowed; the polemical tactics they employed were borrowed in every particular, great and small. Their very frame of mind was borrowed. Borrowing, borrowing, here, there, and everywhere! The single original thing about them was that they invariably made a wrong and unseasonable application of their borrowings.

It can surprise no one that this body, the members of which, as critics, supported themselves by borrowing, should have presupposed similar action on my part, as author. Two, possibly more than two, of the newspapers promptly discovered that I had borrowed this, that, and the other thing form Henrik Hertz's play, *Svend Dyring's House.*

This is a baseless and indefensible critical assertion. It is evidently to be ascribed to the fact that the metre of the ancient ballads is employed in both plays. But my tone is quite different from Hertz's; the language of my play has a different ring; a light summer breeze plays over the rhythm of my verse: over that or Hertz's brood the storms of autumn.

Nor, as regards the characters, the action, and the contents of the plays generally, is there any other or any greater resemblance between them than that which is a natural consequence of the derivation of the subjects of both from the narrow circle of ideas in which the ancient ballads move.

It might be maintained with quite as much, or even more, reason that Hertz in his *Svend Dyring's House* had borrowed, and that to no inconsiderable extent, from Heinrich von Kleist's *Kathchen von Heilbronn*, a play written at the beginning of this century. Kathchen's relation to Count Wetterstrahl is in all essentials the same as Tagnhild's to the knight, Stig Hvide. Like Ragnhild, Kathchen is compelled by a mysterious, inexplicable power to follow the man she loves wherever he goes, to steal secretly after him, to lay herself down to sleep near him, to come back to him, as by some innate

13

compulsion, however often she may be driven away. And other instances of supernatural interference are to be met with both in Kleist's and in Hertz's play.

But does any one doubt that it would be possible, with a little good — or a little ill-will, to discover among still older dramatic literature a play from which it could be maintained that Kleist had borrowed here and there in his *Kathchen von Heilbronn*? I, for my part, do not doubt it. But such suggestions of indebtedness are futile. What makes a work of art the spiritual property of its creator is the fact that he has imprinted on it the stamp of his own personality. Therefore I hold that, in spite of the above-mentioned points of resemblance, *Svend Dyring's House* is as incontestably and entirely an original work by Henrick Hertz as *Katchen von Heilbronn* is an original work by Heinrich von Kleist.

I advance the same claim on my own behalf as regards *The Feast at Solhoug*, and I trust that, for the future, each of the three namesakes* will be permitted to keep, in its entirety, what rightfully belongs to him.

In writing *The Feast of Solhoug* in connection with *Svend Dyring's House*, George Brandes expresses the opinion, not that the former play is founded upon any idea borrowed from the latter, but that it has been written under an influence exercised by the older author upon the younger. Brandes invariably criticises my work in such a friendly spirit that I have all reason to be obliged to him for this suggestion, as for so much else.

Nevertheless I must maintain that he, too, is in this instance mistaken. I have never specially admired Henrik Hertz as a dramatist. Hence it is impossible for me to believe that he should, unknown to myself, have been able to exercise any influence on by dramatic production.

As regards this point and the matter in general, I might confine myself to referring those interested to the writings of Dr. Valfrid Vasenius, lecturer on Aesthetics at the University of Helsingfors. In the thesis which gained him his degree of Doctor of Philosophy, *Henrik Ibsen's Dramatic Poetry in its First stage* (1879), and also in *Henrik Ibsen: The Portrait of a Skald* (Jos. Seligman & Co., Stockholm, 1882), Valsenious states and supports his views on the subject of the play at present in question, supplementing them in the latter work by what I told him, very briefly, when we were together at Munich three years ago.

But, to prevent all misconception, I will now myself give a short account of the origin of *The Feast at Solhoug*.

I began this Preface with the statement that *The Feast at Solhoug* was written in the summer 1855.

In 1854 I had written *Lady Inger of Ostrat*. This was a task which had obliged me to devote much attention to the literature and history of Norway during the Middle Ages, especially the latter part of that period. I did my utmost to familiarise myself with the manners and customs, with the emotions, thought, and language of the men of those days.

The period, however, is not one over which the student is tempted to linger, nor does it present much material suitable for dramatic treatment.

Consequently I soon deserted it for the Saga period. But the Sagas of the Kings, and in general the more strictly historical traditions of that far-off age, did not attract me greatly; at that time I was unable to put the quarrels between kings and chieftains, parties and clans, to any dramatic purpose. This was to happen later.

In the Icelandic "family" Sagas, on the other hand, I found in abundance what I required in the shape of human garb for the moods, conceptions, and thoughts which at that time occupied me, or were, at least, more or less distinctly present in my mind. With these Old Norse contributions to the personal history of our Saga period I had had no previous acquaintance; I had hardly so much as heard them named. But now N. M. Petersen's excellent translation — excellent, at least, as far as the style is concerned — fell into my hands. In the pages of these family chronicles, with their variety of scenes and of relations between man and man, between woman and woman, in short, between human being and human being, there met me a personal, eventful, really living life; and as the result of my intercourse with all these distinctly individual men and women, there presented themselves to my mind's eye the first rough, indistinct outlines of *The Vikings at Helgeland*.

How far the details of that drama then took shape, I am no longer able to say. But I remember perfectly that the two figures of which I first caught sight were the two women who in course of time became Hiordis and Dagny. There was to be a great banquet in the play, with passion-rousing, fateful quarrels during its course. Of other characters and passions, and situations produced by these, I meant to include whatever seemed to me most typical of the life which the Sagas reveal. In short, it was my intention to reproduce dramatically exactly what the Saga of the Volsungs gives in epic form.

I made no complete, connected plan at that time; but it was evident to me that such a drama was to be my first undertaking.

Various obstacles intervened. Most of them were of a personal nature, and these were probably the most decisive; but it undoubtedly had its significance that I happened just at this time to make a careful study of Landstad's collection of Norwegian ballads, published two years previously. My mood of the moment was more in harmony with the literary romanticism of the Middle Ages than with the deeds of the Sagas, with poetical than with prose composition, with the word-melody of the ballad than with the characterisation of the Saga.

Thus it happened that the fermenting, formless design for the tragedy, *The Vikings at Helgeland*, transformed itself temporarily into the lyric drama, *The Feast at Solhoug*.

The two female characters, the foster sisters Hiordis and Dagny, of the projected tragedy, became the sisters Margit and Signe of the completed lyric drama. The derivation of the latter pair from the two women of the Saga at once becomes apparent when attention is drawn to it. The relationship is unmistakable. The tragic hero, so far only vaguely outlined, Sigurd, the far-travelled Viking, the welcome guest at the courts of kings, became the knight and minstrel, Gudmund Alfson, who has likewise been long absent in foreign lands, and has lived in the king's household. His attitude towards the two sisters was changed, to bring it into accordance with the change in time and circumstances; but the position of both sisters to him remained practically the same as that in the projected and afterwards completed tragedy. The fateful banquet, the presentation of which had seemed to me of the first importance in my original plan, became in the drama the scene upon which its personages made their appearance; it became the background against which the action stood out, and communicated to the picture as a whole the general tone at which I aimed. The ending of the play was, undoubtedly, softened and subdued into harmony with its character as drama, not tragedy; but orthodox aestheticians may still, perhaps, find it indisputable whether, in this ending, a touch of pure tragedy has not been left behind, to testify to the origin of the drama.

Upon this subject, however, I shall not enter at present. My object has simply been to maintain and prove that the play under consideration, like all my other dramatic works, is an inevitable outcome of the tenor of my life at a certain period. It had its origin within, and was not the result of any outward impression or influence.

This, and no other, is the true account of the genesis of *The Feast at Solhoug*.

Henrik Ibsen.
Rome, April, 1883.

*Heinrich von Kleist, Henrik Hertz, Henrik Ibsen.

THE FEAST AT SOLHOUG

CHARACTERS

BENGT GAUTESON, Master of Solhoug.
MARGIT, his wife.
SIGNE, her sister.
GUDMUND ALFSON, their kinsman.
KNUT GESLING, the King's sheriff.
ERIK OF HEGGE, his friend.
A HOUSE-CARL.
ANOTHER HOUSE-CARL.
THE KING'S ENVOY.
AN OLD MAN.
A MAIDEN.
GUESTS, both MEN and LADIES.
MEN of KNUT GESLING'S TRAIN.
SERVING-MEN and MAIDENS at SOLHOUG.

The action passes at Solhoug in the Fourteenth Century.

PRONUNCIATION OF NAMES: Gudmund=Goodmund.
The g in "Margit" and in "Gesling" is hard, as in "go," or in
"Gesling," it may be pronounced as y — "Yesling." The first o in
Solhoug ought to have the sound of a very long "oo."

Transcriber's notes:

—Signe and Hegge have umlauts above the e's, the
 ultimate e only in Hegge.
—Passages that are in lyric form are not indented

and have the directorial comments to the right of
the character's name.

THE FEAST AT SOLHOUG

PLAY IN THREE ACTS

ACT FIRST

A stately room, with doors in the back and to both sides. In front on the right, a bay window with small round panes, set in lead, and near the window a table, on which is a quantity of feminine orna-ments. Along the left wall, a longer table with silver goblets and drinking-horns. The door in the back leads out to a passage-way,* through which can be seen a spacious fiord-landscape.

BENGT GAUTESON, MARGIT, KNUT GESLING and ERIK OF HEGGE are seated around the table on the left. In the background are KNUT's followers, some seated, some standing; one or two flag-ons of ale are handed round among them. Far off are heard church bells, ringing to Mass.

*This no doubt means a sort of arcaded veranda running along the outer wall of the house.

ERIK.

[Rising at the table.] In one word, now, what answer have you to make to my wooing on Knut Gesling's behalf?

BENGT.

[Glancing uneasily towards his wife.] Well, I — to me it seems — [As she remains silent.] H'm, Margit, let us first hear your thought in the matter.

MARGIT.

[Rising.] Sir Knut Gesling, I have long known all that Erik of Hegge has told of you. I know full well that you come of a lordly house; you are rich in gold and gear, and you stand in high favour with our royal master.

BENGT.

[To KNUT.] In high favour — so say I too.

MARGIT.

And doubtless my sister could choose her no doughtier mate —

BENGT.

None doughtier; that is what *I* say too.

MARGIT.

— If so be that you can win her to think kindly of you.

BENGT.

[Anxiously, and half aside.] Nay — nay, my dear wife —

KNUT.

[Springing up.] Stands it so, Dame Margit! You think that your sister—

BENGT.

[Seeking to calm him.] Nay, nay, Knut Gesling! Have patience, now. You must understand us aright.

MARGIT.

There is naught in my words to wound you. My sister knows you only by the songs that are made about you—and these songs sound but ill in gentle ears.

No peaceful home is your father's house.
  With your lawless, reckless crew,
Day out, day in, must you hold carouse—
  God help her who mates with you.
God help the maiden you lure or buy
  With gold and with forests green—
Soon will her sore heart long to lie
  Still in the grave, I ween.

ERIK.

Aye, aye—true enough—Knut Gesling lives not overpeaceably. But there will soon come a change in that, when he gets him a wife in his hall.

KNUT.

And this I would have you mark, Dame Margit: it may be a week since, I was at a feast at Hegge, at Erik's bidding, whom here you see. I vowed a vow that Signe, your fair sister, should be my wife, and that before the year was out. Never shall it be said of Knut Gesling that he brake any vow. You can see, then, that you must e'en choose me for your sister's husband — be it with your will or against it.

MARGIT.

Ere that may be, I must tell you plain,
You must rid yourself of your ravening train.
You must scour no longer with yell and shout
O'er the country-side in a galloping rout;
You must still the shudder that spreads around
When Knut Gesling is to a bride-ale bound.
Courteous must your mien be when a-feasting you ride;
Let your battle-axe hang at home at the chimney-side —
It ever sits loose in your hand, well you know,
When the mead has gone round and your brain is aglow.
From no man his rightful gear shall you wrest,
You shall harm no harmless maiden;
You shall send no man the shameless hest
That when his path crosses yours, he were best
Come with his grave-clothes laden.
And if you will so bear you till the year be past,
You may win my sister for your bride at last.

KNUT.

[With suppressed rage.] You know how to order your words cunningly, Dame Margit. Truly, you should have been a priest, and not your husbands wife.

BENGT.

Oh, for that matter, I too could —

KNUT.

[Paying no heed to him.] But I would have you take note that had a sword-bearing man spoken to me in such wise —

BENGT.

Nay, but listen, Knut Gesling — you must understand us!

KNUT.

[As before.] Well, briefly, he should have learnt that the axe sits loose in my hand, as you said but now.

BENGT.

[Softly.] There we have it! Margit, Margit, this will never end well.

MARGIT.

[To KNUT.] You asked for a forthright answer, and that I have given you.

KNUT.

Well, well; I will not reckon too closely with you, Dame Margit. You have more wit than all the rest of us together. Here is my hand; — it may be there was somewhat of reason in the keen-edged words you spoke to me.

MARGIT.

This I like well; now are you already on the right way to amendment. Yet one word more — to-day we hold a feast at Solhoug.

KNUT.

A feast?

BENGT.

Yes, Knut Gesling: you must know that it is our wedding day; this day three years ago made me Dame Margit's husband.

MARGIT.

[Impatiently, interrupting.] As I said, we hold a feast to-day. When Mass is over, and your other business done, I would have you ride hither again, and join in the banquet. Then you can learn to know my sister.

KNUT.

So be it, Dame Margit; I thank you. Yet 'twas not to go to Mass that I rode hither this morning. Your kinsman, Gudmund Alfson, was the cause of my coming.

MARGIT.

[Starts.] He! My kinsman? Where would you seek him?

KNUT.

His homestead lies behind the headland, on the other side of the fiord.

MARGIT.

But he himself is far away.

ERIK.

Be not so sure; he may be nearer than you think.

KNUT.

[Whispers.] Hold your peace!

MARGIT.

Nearer? What mean you?

KNUT.

Have you not heard, then, that Gudmund Alfson has come back to Norway? He came with the Chancellor Audun of Hegranes, who was sent to France to bring home our new Queen.

MARGIT.

True enough, but in these very days the King holds his wedding- feast in full state at Bergen, and there is Gudmund Alfson a guest.

BENGT.

And there could we too have been guests had my wife so willed it.

ERIK.

[Aside to KNUT.] Then Dame Margit knows not that—?

KNUT.

[Aside.] So it would seem; but keep your counsel. [Aloud.] Well, well, Dame Margit, I must go my way none the less, and see what may betide. At nightfall I will be here again.

MARGIT.

And then you must show whether you have power to bridle your unruly spirit.

BENGT.

Aye, mark you that.

MARGIT.

You must lay no hand on your axe—hear you, Knut Gesling?

BENGT.

Neither on your axe, nor on your knife, nor on any other weapon whatsoever.

MARGIT.

For then can you never hope to be one of our kindred.

BENGT.

Nay, that is our firm resolve.

KNUT.

[To MARGIT.] Have no fear.

BENGT.

And what we have firmly resolved stands fast.

KNUT.

That I like well, Sir Bengt Gauteson. I, too, say the same; and
I have pledged myself at the feast-board to wed your kinswoman.
You may be sure that my pledge, too, will stand fast. — God's peace
till to-night!

[He and ERIK, with their men, go out at the back.
[BENGT accompanies them to the door. The sound of the bells
has in the meantime ceased.

BENGT.

[Returning.] Methought he seemed to threaten us as he departed.

MARGIT.

[Absently.] Aye, so it seemed.

BENGT.

Knut Gesling is an ill man to fall out with. And when I bethink
me, we gave him over many hard words. But come, let us not brood
over that. To-day we must be merry, Margit! — as I trow we have
both good reason to be.

MARGIT.

[With a weary smile.] Aye, surely, surely.

BENGT.

Tis true I was no mere stripling when I courted you. But well I wot I was the richest man for many and many a mile. You were a fair maiden, and nobly born; but your dowry would have tempted no wooer.

MARGIT.

[To herself.] Yet was I then so rich.

BENGT.

What said you, my wife?

MARGIT.

Oh, nothing, nothing. [Crosses to the right.] I will deck me with pearls and rings. Is not to-night a time of rejoicing for me?

BENGT.

I am fain to hear you say it. Let me see that you deck you in your best attire, that our guests may say: Happy she who mated with Bengt Gauteson. — But now must I to the larder; there are many things to-day that must not be over-looked.

[He goes out to the left.

MARGIT. [Sinks down on a chair by the table on the right.]

'Twas well he departed. While here he remains
Meseems the blood freezes within my veins;
Meseems that a crushing mighty and cold
My heart in its clutches doth still enfold.
　　[With tears she cannot repress.

He is my husband! I am his wife!
How long, how long lasts a woman's life?
Sixty years, mayhap—God pity me
Who am not yet full twenty-three!
     [More calmly after a short silence.

Hard, so long in a gilded cage to pine;
Hard a hopeless prisoner's lot—and mine.
     [Absently fingering the ornaments on the table, and beginning
        to put them on.

With rings, and with jewels, and all of my best
By his order myself I am decking—
But oh, if to-day were my burial-feast,
'Twere little that I'd be recking.
     [Breaking off.

But if thus I brood I must needs despair;
I know a song that can lighten care.
     [She sings.

The Hill-King to the sea did ride;
     —Oh, sad are my days and dreary—
To woo a maiden to be his bride.
     —I am waiting for thee, I am weary.—

The Hill-King rode to Sir Hakon's hold;
     —Oh, sad are my days and dreary—
Little Kirsten sat combing her locks of gold.
     —I am waiting for thee, I am weary.—

The Hill-King wedded the maiden fair;
     —Oh, sad are my days and dreary—
A silvern girdle she ever must wear.
     —I am waiting for thee, I am weary.—

The Hill-King wedded the lily-wand,
  —Oh, sad are my days and dreary—
With fifteen gold rings on either hand.
  —I am waiting for thee, I am weary.—

Three summers passed, and there passed full five;
  —Oh, sad are my days and dreary—
In the hill little Kirsten was buried alive.
  —I am waiting for thee, I am weary.—

Five summers passed, and there passed full nine;
  —Oh, sad are my days and dreary—
Little Kirsten ne'er saw the glad sunshine.
  —I am waiting for thee, I am weary.—

In the dale there are flowers and the birds' blithe song;
  —Oh, sad are my days and dreary—
In the hill there is gold and the night is long.
  —I am waiting for thee, I am weary.—
    [She rises and crosses the room.

How oft in the gloaming would Gudmund sing
This song in may father's hall.
There was somewhat in it—some strange, sad thing
That took my heart in thrall;
Though I scarce understood, I could ne'er forget—
And the words and the thoughts they haunt me yet.
    [Stops horror-struck.

Rings of red gold! And a belt beside—!
'Twas with gold the Hill-King wedded his bride!
    [In despair; sinks down on a bench beside the table on
      the left.

Woe! Woe! I myself am the Hill-King's wife!
And there cometh none to free me from the prison of my life.

    [SIGNE, radiant with gladness, comes running in from
      the back.

SIGNE.

    [Calling.] Margit, Margit, — he is coming!

MARGIT.

    [Starting up.] Coming? Who is coming?

SIGNE.

    Gudmund, our kinsman!

MARGIT.

    Gudmund Alfson! Here! How can you think — ?

SIGNE.

    Oh, I am sure of it.

MARGIT.

    [Crosses to the right.] Gudmund Alfson is at the wedding-feast in the King's hall; you know that as well as I.

SIGNE.

    Maybe; but none the less I am sure it was he.

MARGIT.

Have you seen him?

SIGNE.

Oh, no, no; but I must tell you —

MARGIT.

Yes, haste you — tell on!

SIGNE.

'Twas early morn, and the church bells rang,
To Mass I was fain to ride;
The birds in the willows twittered and sang,
In the birch-groves far and wide.
All earth was glad in the clear, sweet day;
And from church it had well-nigh stayed me;
For still, as I rode down the shady way,
Each rosebud beguiled and delayed me.
Silently into the church I stole;
The priest at the altar was bending;
He chanted and read, and with awe in their soul,
The folk to God's word were attending.
Then a voice rang out o'er the fiord so blue;
And the carven angels, the whole church through,
Turned round, methought, to listen thereto.

MARGIT.

O Signe, say on! Tell me all, tell me all!

SIGNE.

'Twas as though a strange, irresistible call
Summoned me forth from the worshipping flock,
Over hill and dale, over mead and rock.
'Mid the silver birches I listening trod,
Moving as though in a dream;
Behind me stood empty the house of God;
Priest and people were lured by the magic 'twould seem,
Of the tones that still through the air did stream.
No sound they made; they were quiet as death;
To hearken the song-birds held their breath,
The lark dropped earthward, the cuckoo was still,
As the voice re-echoed from hill to hill.

MARGIT.

Go on.

SIGNE.

They crossed themselves, women and men;
      [Pressing her hands to her breast.

But strange thoughts arose within me then;
For the heavenly song familiar grew:
Gudmund oft sang it to me and you —
Ofttimes has Gudmund carolled it,
And all he e'er sang in my heart is writ.

MARGIT.

And you think that it may be — ?

SIGNE.

I know it is he! I know it? I know it! You soon shall see!
   [Laughing.

From far-off lands, at the last, in the end,
Each song-bird homeward his flight doth bend!
I am so happy — though why I scarce know — !
Margit, what say you? I'll quickly go
And take down his harp, that has hung so long
In there on the wall that 'tis rusted quite;
Its golden strings I will polish bright,
And tune them to ring and to sing with his song.

  MARGIT. [Absently.]

Do as you will —

  SIGNE. [Reproachfully.]

   Nay, this in not right.
  [Embracing her.

But when Gudmund comes will your heart grow light —
Light, as when I was a child, again.

MARGIT.

  So much has changed — ah, so much! — since then —

SIGNE.

Margit, you shall be happy and gay!
Have you not serving-maids many, and thralls?

Costly robes hang in rows on your chamber walls;
How rich you are, none can say.
By day you can ride in the forest deep,
Chasing the hart and the hind;
By night in a lordly bower you can sleep,
On pillows of silk reclined.

MARGIT. [Looking toward the window.]

And he comes to Solhoug! He, as a guest!

SIGNE.

What say you?

MARGIT. [Turning.]

Naught. — Deck you out in your best.
That fortune which seemeth to you so bright
May await yourself.

SIGNE.

Margit, say what you mean!

MARGIT. [Stroking her hair.]

I mean — nay, no more! 'Twill shortly be seen — ;
I mean — should a wooer ride hither to-night — ?

SIGNE.

A wooer? For whom?

MARGIT.

For you.

SIGNE. [Laughing.]

For me?
That he'd ta'en the wrong road full soon he would see.

MARGIT.

What would you say if a valiant knight
Begged for your hand?

SIGNE.

That my heart was too light
To think upon suitors or choose a mate.

MARGIT.

But if he were mighty, and rich, and great?

SIGNE.

O, were he a king, did his palace hold
Stores of rich garments and ruddy gold,
'Twould ne'er set my heart desiring.
With you I am rich enough here, meseeems,
With summer and sun and the murmuring streams,
And the birds in the branches quiring.
Dear sister mine — here shall my dwelling be;
And to give any wooer my hand in fee,

For that I am too busy, and my heart too full of glee!

[SIGNE runs out to the left, singing.

MARGIT.

[After a pause.] Gudmund Alfson coming hither! Hither—to Solhoug? No, no, it cannot be.—Signe heard him singing, she said! When I have heard the pine-trees moaning in the forest afar, when I have heard the waterfall thunder and the birds pipe their lure in the tree-tops, it has many a time seemed to me as though, through it all, the sound of Gudmund's songs came blended. And yet he was far from here.—Signe has deceived herself. Gudmund cannot be coming.

[BENGT enters hastily from the back.

BENGT.

[Entering, calls loudly.] An unlooked-for guest my wife!

MARGIT.

What guest?

BENGT.

Your kinsman, Gudmund Alfson! [Calls through the doorway on the right.] Let the best guest-room be prepared—and that forthwith!

MARGIT.

Is he, then, already here?

BENGT.

[Looking out through the passage-way.] Nay, not yet; but he cannot be far off. [Calls again to the right.] The carved oak bed, with the dragon-heads! [Advances to MARGIT.] His shield- bearer brings a message of greeting from him; and he himself is close behind.

MARGIT.

His shield-bearer! Comes he hither with a shield-bearer!

BENGT.

Aye, by my faith he does. He has a shield-bearer and six armed men in his train. What would you? Gudmund Alfson is a far other man than he was when he set forth to seek his fortune. But I must ride forth to seek him. [Calls out.] The gilded saddle on my horse! And forget not the bridle with the serpents' heads! [Looks out to the back.] Ha, there he is already at the gate! Well, then, my staff—my silver-headed staff! Such a lordly knight—Heaven save us!—we must receive him with honour, with all seemly honour!

[Goes hastily out to the back.

MARGIT. [Brooding]

Alone he departed, a penniless swain;
With esquires and henchmen now comes he again.
What would he? Comes he, forsooth, to see
My bitter and gnawing misery?
Would he try how long, in my lot accurst,
I can writhe and moan, ere my heart-strings burst—
Thinks he that—? Ah, let him only try!
Full little joy shall he reap thereby.
  [She beckons through the doorway on the right. Three
    handmaidens enter.

List, little maids, what I say to you:
Find me my silken mantle blue.
Go with me into my bower anon:
My richest of velvets and furs do on.
Two of you shall deck me in scarlet and vair,
The third shall wind pearl-strings into my hair.
All my jewels and gauds bear away with ye!
   [The handmaids go out to the left, taking the ornaments
     with them.

Since Margit the Hill-King's bride must be,
Well! don we the queenly livery!

   [She goes out to the left.
   [BENGT ushers in GUDMUND ALFSON, through the pent-
house
    passage at the back.

BENGT.

   And now once more—welcome under Solhoug's roof, my wife's kinsman.

GUDMUND.

   I thank you. And how goes it with her? She thrives well in every way, I make no doubt?

BENGT.

   Aye, you may be sure she does. There is nothing she lacks. She has five handmaidens, no less, at her beck and call; a courser stands ready saddled in the stall when she lists to ride abroad. In one word, she has all that a noble lady can desire to make her happy in her lot.

GUDMUND.

And Margit—is she then happy?

BENGT.

God and all men would think that she must be; but, strange to say—

GUDMUND.

What mean you?

BENGT.

Well, believe it or not as you list, but it seems to me that Margit was merrier of heart in the days of her poverty, than since she became the lady of Solhoug.

GUDMUND.

[To himself.] I knew it; so it must be.

BENGT.

What say you, kinsman?

GUDMUND.

I say that I wonder greatly at what you tell me of your wife.

BENGT.

Aye, you may be sure I wonder at it too. On the faith and troth of an honest gentleman, 'tis beyond me to guess what more she can desire. I am about her all day long; and no one can say of me that I rule her harshly. All the cares of household and husbandry I have taken on myself; yet notwithstanding— Well, well, you were ever a merry heart; I doubt not you will bring sunshine with you. Hush! here comes Dame Margit! Let her not see that I—

[MARGIT enters from the left, richly dressed.

GUDMUND.

[Going to meet her.] Margit—my dear Margit!

MARGIT.

[Stops, and looks at him without recognition.] Your pardon, Sir Knight; but—? [As though she only now recognized him.] Surely, if I mistake not, 'tis Gudmund Alfson.

[Holding out her hand to him.

GUDMUND.

[Without taking it.] And you did not at once know me again?

BENGT.

[Laughing.] Why, Margit, of what are you thinking? I told you but a moment agone that your kinsman—

MARGIT.

[Crossing to the table on the right.] Twelve years is a long time, Gudmund. The freshest plant may wither ten times over in that space.

GUDMUND.

'Tis seven years since last we met.

43

MARGIT.

Surely it must be more than that.

GUDMUND.

[Looking at her.] I could almost think so. But 'tis as I say.

MARGIT.

How strange! I must have been but a child then; and it seems to me a whole eternity since I was a child. [Throws herself down on a chair.] Well, sit you down, my kinsman! Rest you, for to-night you shall dance, and rejoice us with your singing. [With a forced smile.] Doubtless you know we are merry here to-day — we are holding a feast.

GUDMUND.

'Twas told me as I entered your homestead.

BENGT.

Aye, 'tis three years to-day since I became —

MARGIT.

[Interrupting.] My kinsman has already heard it. [To GUDMUND.] Will you not lay aside your cloak?

GUDMUND.

I thank you, Dame Margit; but it seems to me cold here — colder than I had foreseen.

BENGT.

For my part, I am warm enough; but then I have a hundred things to do and to take order for. [To MARGIT.] Let not the time seem long to our guest while I am absent. You can talk together of the old days.

[Going.

MARGIT.

[Hesitating.] Are you going? Will you not rather—?

BENGT.

[Laughing, to GUDMUND, as he comes forward again.] See you well— Sir Bengt of Solhoug is the man to make the women fain of him. How short so e'er the space, my wife cannot abide to be without me. [To MARGIT, caressing her.] Content you; I shall soon be with you again.

[He goes out to the back.

MARGIT.

[To herself.] Oh, torture, to have to endure it all.

[A short silence.

GUDMUND.

How goes it, I pray, with your sister dear?

MARGIT.

Right well, I thank you.

GUDMUND.

They said she was here
With you.

MARGIT.

She has been here ever since we —
[Breaks off.

She came, now three years since, to Solhoug with me.
[After a pause.

Ere long she'll be here, her friend to greet.

GUDMUND.

Well I mind me of Signe's nature sweet.
No guile she dreamed of, no evil knew.
When I call to remembrance her eyes so blue
I must think of the angels in heaven.
But of years there have passed no fewer than seven;
In that time much may have altered. Oh, say
If she, too, has changed so while I've been away?

MARGIT.

She too? Is it, pray, in the halls of kings
That you learn such courtly ways, Sir Knight?
To remind me thus of the change time brings —

GUDMUND.

Nay, Margit, my meaning you read aright!
You were kind to me, both, in those far-away years —
Your eyes, when we parted were wet with tears.
We swore like brother and sister still
To hold together in good hap or ill.
'Mid the other maids like a sun you shone,
Far, far and wide was your beauty known.
You are no less fair than you were, I wot;
But Solhoug's mistress, I see, has forgot
The penniless kinsman. So hard is your mind
That ever of old was gentle and kind.

MARGIT. [Choking back her tears.]

Aye, of old —!

GUDMUND. [Looks compassionately at her, is silent for a little, then says in a subdued voice.

Shall we do as your husband said?
Pass the time with talk of the dear old days?

MARGIT. [Vehemently.]

No, no, not of them!
Their memory's dead.
My mind unwillingly backward strays.
Tell rather of what your life has been,
Of what in the wide world you've done and seen.
Adventures you've lacked not, well I ween —
In all the warmth and the space out yonder,
That heart and mind should be light, what wonder?

GUDMUND.

In the King's high hall I found not the joy
That I knew by my own poor hearth as a boy.

MARGIT. [Without looking at him.]

While I, as at Solhoug each day flits past,
Thank Heaven that here has my lot been cast.

GUDMUND.

'Tis well if for this you can thankful be—

MARGIT. [Vehemently.]

Why not? For am I not honoured and free?
Must not all folk here obey my hest?
Rule I not all things as seemeth me best?
Here I am first, with no second beside me;
And that, as you know, from of old satisfied me.
Did you think you would find me weary and sad?
Nay, my mind is at peace and my heart is glad.
You might, then, have spared your journey here
To Solhoug; 'twill profit you little, I fear.

GUDMUND.

What, mean you, Dame Margit?

MARGIT. [Rising.]

                I understand all —
I know why you come to my lonely hall.

GUDMUND.

And you welcome me not, though you know why I came?
    [Bowing and about to go.

    God's peace and farewell, then, my noble dame!

MARGIT.

To have stayed in the royal hall, indeed,
Sir Knight, had better become your fame.

        GUDMUND. [Stops.]

    In the royal hall? Do you scoff at my need?

MARGIT.

Your need? You are ill to content, my friend;
Where, I would know, do you think to end?
You can dress you in velvet and cramoisie,
You stand by the throne, and have lands in fee —

GUDMUND.

Do you deem, then, that fortune is kind to me?
You said but now that full well you knew
What brought me to Solhoug —

MARGIT.

I told you true!

GUDMUND.

Then you know what of late has befallen me; —
You have heard the tale of my outlawry?

MARGIT. [Terror-struck.]

An outlaw! You, Gudmund!

GUDMUND.

I am indeed.
But I swear, by the Holy Christ I swear,
Had I known the thoughts of your heart, I ne'er
Had bent me to Solhoug in my need.
I thought that you still were gentle-hearted,
As you ever were wont to be ere we parted:
But I truckle not to you; the wood is wide,
My hand and my bow shall fend for me there;
I will drink of the mountain brook, and hide
My head in the beast's lair.

[On the point of going.

MARGIT. [Holding him back.]

Outlawed! Nay, stay! I swear to you
That naught of your outlawry I knew.

GUDMUND.

It is as I tell you. My life's at stake;
And to live are all men fain.
Three nights like a dog 'neath the sky I've lain,
My couch on the hillside forced to make,
With for pillow the boulder grey.
Though too proud to knock at the door of the stranger,
And pray him for aid in the hour of danger,
Yet strong was my hope as I held on my way:
I thought: When to Solhoug you come at last
Then all your pains will be done and past.
You have sure friends there, whatever betide. —
But hope like a wayside flower shrivels up;
Though your husband met me with flagon and cup,
And his doors flung open wide,
Within, your dwelling seems chill and bare;
Dark is the hall; my friends are not there.
'Tis well; I will back to my hills from your halls.

MARGIT. [Beseechingly.]

Oh, hear me!

GUDMUND.

My soul is not base as a thrall's.
Now life to me seems a thing of nought;
Truly I hold it scarce worth a thought.
You have killed all that I hold most dear;
Of my fairest hopes I follow the bier.
Farewell, then, Dame Margit!

MARGIT.

Nay, Gudmund, hear!
By all that is holy—!

GUDMUND.

Live on as before
Live on in honour and joyance—
Never shall Gudmund darken your door,
Never shall cause you 'noyance.

MARGIT.

Enough, enough. Your bitterness
You presently shall rue.
Had I known you outlawed, shelterless,
Hunted the country through—
Trust me, the day that brought you here
Would have seemed the fairest of many a year;
And a feast I had counted it indeed
When you turned to Solhoug for refuge in need.

GUDMUND.

What say you—? How shall I read your mind?

MARGIT. [Holding out her hand to him.]

Read this: that at Solhoug dwell kinsfolk kind.

GUDMUND.

But you said of late—?

MARGIT.

> To that pay no heed,
Or hear me, and understand indeed.
For me is life but a long, black night,
Nor sun, nor star for me shines bright.
I have sold my youth and my liberty,
And none from my bargain can set me free.
My heart's content I have bartered for gold,
With gilded chains I have fettered myself;
Trust me, it is but comfort cold
To the sorrowful soul, the pride of pelf.
How blithe was my childhood—how free from care!
Our house was lowly and scant our store;
But treasures of hope in my breast I bore.

GUDMUND. [Whose eyes have been fixed upon her.]

E'en then you were growing to beauty rare.

MARGIT.

Mayhap; but the praises showered on me
Caused the wreck of my happiness—that I now see.
To far-off lands away you sailed;
But deep in my heart was graven each song
You had ever sung; and their glamour was strong;
With a mist of dreams my brow they veiled.
In them all the joys you had dwelt upon
That can find a home in the beating breast;
You had sung so oft of the lordly life
'Mid knights and ladies. And lo! anon
Came wooers a many from east and from west;
And so—I became Bengt Gauteson's wife.

GUDMUND.

Oh, Margit!

MARGIT.

The days that passed were but few
Ere with tears my folly I 'gan to rue.
To think, my kinsman and friend, on thee
Was all the comfort left to me.
How empty now seemed Solhoug's hall,
How hateful and drear its great rooms all!
Hither came many a knight and dame,
Came many a skald to sing my fame.
But never a one who could fathom aright
My spirit and all its yearning —
I shivered, as though in the Hill-King's might;
Yet my head throbbed, my blood was burning.

GUDMUND.

But your husband — ?

MARGIT.

He never to me was dear.
'Twas his gold was my undoing.
When he spoke to me, aye, or e'en drew near,
My spirit writhed with ruing.
    [Clasping her hands.

And thus have I lived for three long years —
A life of sorrow, of unstanched tears!
Your coming was rumoured. You know full well
What pride deep down in my heart doth dwell.
I hid my anguish, I veiled my woe,

For you were the last that the truth must know.

GUDMUND. [Moved.]

'Twas therefore, then, that you turned away —

MARGIT. [Not looking at him.]

I thought you came at my woe to jeer.

GUDMUND.

Margit, how could you think —?

MARGIT.

Nay, nay,
There was reason enough for such a fear.
But thanks be to Heaven that fear is gone;
And now no longer I stand alone;
My spirit now is as light and free
As a child's at play 'neath the greenwood tree.
    [With a sudden start of fear.

Ah, where are my wits fled! How could I forget —?
Ye saints, I need sorely your succor yet!
An outlaw, you said —?

GUDMUND. [Smiling.]

Nay, now I'm at home;
Hither the King's men scarce dare come.

MARGIT.

Your fall has been sudden. I pray you, tell
How you lost the King's favour.

GUDMUND.

           'Twas thus it befell.
You know how I journeyed to France of late,
When the Chancellor, Audun of Hegranes,
Fared thither from Bergen, in royal state,
To lead home the King's bride, the fair Princess,
With her squires, and maidens, and ducats bright.
Sir Audun's a fair and stately knight,
The Princess shone with a beauty rare—
Her eyes seemed full of a burning prayer.
They would oft talk alone and in whispers, the two—
Of what? That nobody guessed or knew.
There came a night when I leant at ease
Against the galley's railing;
My thought flew onward to Norway's leas,
With the milk-white seagulls sailing.
Two voices whispered behind my back;—
I turned—it was he and she;
I knew them well, though the night was black,
But they—they saw not me.
She gazed upon him with sorrowful eyes
And whispered: "Ah, if to southern skies
We could turn the vessel's prow,
And we were alone in the bark, we twain,
My heart, methinks, would find peace again,
Nor would fever burn my brow."
Sir Audun answers; and straight she replies,
In words so fierce, so bold;
Like glittering stars I can see her eyes;
She begged him—
    [Breaking off.

My blood ran cold.

MARGIT.

She begged —?

GUDMUND.

I arose, and they vanished apace;
All was silent, fore and aft: —
    [Producing a small phial.

But this I found by their resting place.

MARGIT.

And that —?

GUDMUND. [Lowering his voice.]

        Holds a secret draught.
A drop of this in your enemy's cup
And his life will sicken and wither up.
No leechcraft helps 'gainst the deadly thing.

MARGIT.

And that —?

GUDMUND.

That draught was meant for the King.

MARGIT.

Great God!

GUDMUND. [Putting up the phial again.]

That I found it was well for them all.
In three days more was our voyage ended;
Then I fled, by my faithful men attended.
For I knew right well, in the royal hall,
That Audun subtly would work my fall,—
Accusing me—

MARGIT.

Aye, but at Solhoug he
Cannot harm you. All as of old will be.

GUDMUND.

All? Nay, Margit—you then were free.

MARGIT.

You mean—?

GUDMUND.

I? Nay, I meant naught. My brain
Is wildered; but ah, I am blithe and fain
To be, as of old, with you sisters twain.
But tell me,—Signe—?

MARGIT. [Points smiling towards the door on the left.]

>She comes anon.
To greet her kinsman she needs must don
Her trinkets—a task that takes time, 'tis plain.

GUDMUND.

I must see—I must see if she knows me again.

[He goes out to the left.

MARGIT.

[Following him with her eyes.] How fair and manlike he is! [With a sigh.] There is little likeness 'twixt him and— [Begins putting things in order on the table, but presently stops.] "You then were free," he said. Yes, then! [A short pause.] 'Twas a strange tale, that of the Princess who— She held another dear, and then— Aye, those women of far-off lands— I have heard it before—they are not weak as we are; they do not fear to pass from thought to deed. [Takes up a goblet which stands on the table.] 'Twas in this beaker that Gudmund and I, when he went away, drank to his happy return. 'Tis well-nigh the only heirloom I brought with me to Solhoug. [Putting the goblet away in a cupboard.] How soft is this summer day; and how light it is in here! So sweetly has the sun not shone for three long years.

[SIGNE, and after her GUDMUND, enters from the left.

SIGNE. [Runs laughing up to MARGIT.]
Ha, ha, ha! He will not believe that 'tis I!

MARGIT. [Smiling to GUDMUND.]

You see: while in far-off lands you strayed,
She, too, has altered, the little maid.

GUDMUND.

Aye truly! But that she should be — Why,
'Tis a marvel in very deed.
    [Takes both SIGNE's hands and looks at her.

Yet, when I look in these eyes so blue,
The innocent child-mind I still can read —
Yes, Signe, I know that 'tis you!
I needs must laugh when I think how oft
I have thought of you perched on my shoulder aloft
As you used to ride. You were then a child;
Now you are a nixie, spell-weaving, wild.

SIGNE. [Threatening with her finger.]

Beware! If the nixie's ire you awaken,
Soon in her nets you will find yourself taken.

GUDMUND. [To himself.]

I am snared already, it seems to me.

SIGNE.

But, Gudmund, wait — you have still to see
How I've shielded your harp from the dust and the rust.
    [As she goes out to the left.

You shall teach me all of your songs! You must!

GUDMUND. [Softly, as he follows her with his eyes.]

She has flushed to the loveliest rose of May,
That was yet but a bud in the morning's ray.

SIGNE. [Returning with the harp.]
Behold!

GUDMUND. [Taking it.]

My harp! As bright as of yore!
[Striking one or two chords.

Still the old chords ring sweet and clear —
On the wall, untouched, thou shalt hang no more.

MARGIT. [Looking out at the back.]
Our guests are coming.

SIGNE. [While GUDMUND preludes his song.]
Hush — hush! Oh, hear!

GUDMUND. [Sings.]

I roamed through the uplands so heavy of cheer;
The little birds quavered in bush and in brere;
The little birds quavered, around and above:
Wouldst know of the sowing and growing of love?

It grows like the oak tree through slow-rolling years;
'Tis nourished by dreams, and by songs, and by tears;

But swiftly 'tis sown; ere a moment speeds by,
Deep, deep in the heart love is rooted for aye.

> [As he strikes the concluding chords, he goes towards the
> back where he lays down his harp.

SIGNE. [Thoughtfully, repeats to herself.]

But swiftly 'tis sown; ere a moment speeds by,
Deep, deep in the heart love is rooted for aye.

MARGIT.

[Absently.] Did you speak to me? — I heard not clearly — ?

SIGNE.

I? No, no. I only meant —

[She again becomes absorbed in dreams.

MARGIT. [Half aloud; looking straight before her.]

It grows like the oak tree through slow-rolling years;
'Tis nourished by dreams, and by songs and by tears.

SIGNE.

[Returning to herself.] You said that — ?

MARGIT.

[Drawing her hand over her brow.] Nay, 'twas nothing. Come, we must go meet our guests.

[BENGT enters with many GUESTS, both men and women, through the passageway.

GUESTS.

With song and harping enter we
    The feast-hall opened wide;
Peace to our hostess kind and free,
    All happiness to her betide.
O'er Solhoug's roof for ever may
    Bright as to-day
    The heavens abide.

ACT SECOND

A birch grove adjoining the house, one corner of which is seen to the left. At the back, a footpath leads up the hillside. To the right of the footpath a river comes tumbling down a ravine and loses itself among boulders and stones. It is a light summer evening. The door leading to the house stands open; the windows are lighted up. Music is heard from within.

THE GUESTS. [Singing in the Feast Hall.]

Set bow to fiddle! To sound of strings
We'll dance till night shall furl her wings,
  Through the long hours glad and golden!
Like blood-red blossom the maiden glows —
Come, bold young wooer and hold the rose
  In a soft embrace enfolden.

[KNUT GESLING and ERIK OF HEGGE enter from the house. Sounds of music, dancing and merriment are heard from within during what follows.

ERIK.

If only you come not to repent it, Knut.

KNUT.

That is my affair.

ERIK.

Well, say what you will, 'tis a daring move. You are the King's Sheriff. Commands go forth to you that you shall seize the person of Gudmund Alfson, wherever you may find him. And now, when you have him in your grasp, you proffer him your friendship, and let him go freely, whithersoever he will.

KNUT.

I know what I am doing. I sought him in his own dwelling, but there he was not to be found. If, now, I went about to seize him here—think you that Dame Margit would be minded to give me Signe to wife?

ERIK.

[With deliberation.] No, by fair means it might scarcely be, but—

KNUT.

And by foul means I am loth to proceed. Moreover, Gudmund is my friend from bygone days; and he can be helpful to me. [With decision.] Therefore it shall be as I have said. This evening no one at Solhoug shall know that Gudmund Alfson is an outlaw;— to-morrow he must look to himself.

ERIK.

Aye, but the King's decree?

KNUT.

Oh, the King's decree! You know as well as I that the King's decree is but little heeded here in the uplands. Were the King's decree to be enforced, many a stout fellow among us would have to pay dear both for bride-rape and for man-slaying. Come this way, I would fain know where Signe—?

[They go out to the right.
[GUDMUND and SIGNE come down the footpath at the back.

SIGNE.

Oh, speak! Say on! For sweeter far
Such words than sweetest music are.

GUDMUND.

Signe, my flower, my lily fair!

SIGNE. [In subdued, but happy wonderment.]

I am dear to him—I!

Gudmund.

As none other I swear.

SIGNE.

And is it I that can bind your will!
And is it I that your heart can fill!
Oh, dare I believe you?

GUDMUND.

Indeed you may.
List to me, Signe! The years sped away,
But faithful was I in my thoughts to you,

My fairest flowers, ye sisters two.
My own heart I could not clearly read.
When I left, my Signe was but a child,
A fairy elf, like the creatures wild
Who play, while we sleep, in wood and mead.
But in Solhoug's hall to-day, right loud
My heart spake, and right clearly;
It told me that Margit's a lady proud,
Whilst you're the sweet maiden I love most dearly.

SIGNE. [Who has only half listened to his words.]

I mind me, we sat in the hearth's red glow,
One winter evening — 'tis long ago —
And you sang to me of the maiden fair
Whom the neckan had lured to his watery lair.
There she forgot both father and mother,
There she forgot both sister and brother;
Heaven and earth and her Christian speech,
And her God, she forgot them all and each.
But close by the strand a stripling stood
And he was heartsore and heavy of mood.
He struck from his harpstrings notes of woe,
That wide o'er the waters rang loud, rang low.
The spell-bound maid in the tarn so deep,
His strains awoke from her heavy sleep,
The neckan must grant her release from his rule,
She rose through the lilies afloat on the pool —
Then looked she to heaven while on green earth she trod,
And wakened once more to her faith and her God.

GUDMUND.

Signe, my fairest of flowers!

SIGNE.

                    It seems
That I, too, have lived in a world of dreams.
But the strange deep words you to-night have spoken,
Of the power of love, have my slumber broken.
The heavens seemed never so blue to me,
Never the world so fair;
I can understand, as I roam with thee,
The song of the birds in air.

GUDMUND.

So mighty is love — it stirs in the breast
Thought and longings and happy unrest.
But come, let us both to your sister go.

SIGNE.

Would you tell her — ?

GUDMUND.

Everything she must know.

SIGNE.

Then go you alone; — I feel that my cheek
Would be hot with blushes to hear you speak.

GUDMUND.

So be it, I go.

SIGNE.

And here will I bide;
[Listening towards the right.

Or better — down by the riverside,
I hear Knut Gesling, with maidens and men.

GUDMUND.

There will you stay?

SIGNE.

Till you come again

[She goes out to the right. GUDMUND goes into the house.
[MARGIT enters from behind the house on the left.

MARGIT.

In the hall there is gladness and revelry;
The dancers foot it with jest and glee.
The air weighed hot on my brow and breast;
For Gudmund, he was not there.
[She draws a deep breath.

Out here 'tis better: here's quiet and rest.
How sweet is the cool night air!
[A brooding silence.

The horrible thought! Oh, why should it be
That wherever I go it follows me?
The phial — doth a secret contain;
A drop of this in my — enemy's cup,

And his life would sicken and wither up;
The leech's skill would be tried in vain.
    [Again a silence.

Were I sure that Gudmund — held me dear —
Then little I'd care for —

    [GUDMUND enters from the house.

GUDMUND.

             You, Margit, here?
And alone? I have sought you everywhere.

MARGIT.

'Tis cool here. I sickened of heat and glare.
See you how yonder the white mists glide
Softly over the marshes wide?
Here it is neither dark nor light,
But midway between them —
    [To herself.

             — as in my breast.
    [Looking at him.

Is't not so — when you wander on such a night
You hear, though but half to yourself confessed,
A stirring of secret life through the hush,
In tree and in leaf, in flower and in rush?
    [With a sudden change of tone.

  Can you guess what I wish?

GUDMUND.

Well?

MARGIT.

That I could be
The nixie that haunts yonder upland lea.
How cunningly I should weave my spell!
Trust me — !

GUDMUND.

Margit, what ails you? Tell!

MARGIT. [Paying no heed to him.]

How I should quaver my magic lay!
Quaver and croon it both night and day!
   [With growing vehemence.

How I would lure the knight so bold
Through the greenwood glades to my mountain hold.
There were the world and its woes forgot
In the burning joys of our blissful lot.

GUDMUND.

Margit! Margit!

MARGIT. [Ever more wildly.]

At midnight's hour
Sweet were our sleep in my lonely bower; —

And if death should come with the dawn, I trow
'Twere sweet to die so; — what thinkest thou?

GUDMUND.

You are sick!

MARGIT. [Bursting into laughter.]

Ha, ha! — Let me laugh! 'Tis good
To laugh when the heart is in laughing mood!

GUDMUND.

I see that you still have the same wild soul
As of old —

MARGIT. [With sudden seriousness.]

Nay, let not that vex your mind,
'Tis only at midnight it mocks control;
By day I am timid as any hind.
How tame I have grown, you yourself must say,
When you think on the women in lands far away —
Of that fair Princess — ah, she was wild!
Beside her lamblike am I and mild.
She did not helplessly yearn and brood,
She would have acted; and that —

GUDMUND.

'Tis good
You remind me; Straightway I'll cast away
What to me is valueless after this day —

[Takes out the phial.

MARGIT.

The phial! You meant — ?

GUDMUND.

I thought it might be
At need a friend that should set me free
Should the King's men chance to lay hands on me.
But from to-night it has lost its worth;
Now will I fight all the kings of earth,
Gather my kinsfolk and friends to the strife,
And battle right stoutly for freedom and life.

[Is about to throw the phial against a rock.

MARGIT. [Seizing his arm.]

Nay, hold! Let me have it —

GUDMUND.

First tell me why?

MARGIT.

I'd fain fling it down to the neckan hard by,
Who so often has made my dull hours fleet

With his harping and songs, so strange and sweet.
Give it me!
    [Takes the phial from his hand.

  There!

  [Feigns to throw it into the river.

  GUDMUND. [Goes to the right, and looks down into the ravine.]

  Have you thrown it away?

  MARGIT. [Concealing the phial.]

Aye, surely! You saw —
    [Whispers as she goes towards the house.

       Now God help and spare me!
  [Aloud.

  Gudmund!

  GUDMUND. [Approaching.]

  What would you?

MARGIT.

      Teach me, I pray,
How to interpret the ancient lay
They sing of the church in the valley there:
A gentle knight and a lady fair,
They loved each other well.
That very day on her bier she lay
He on his sword-point fell.
They buried her by the northward spire,

And him by the south kirk wall;
And theretofore grew neither bush nor briar
In the hallowed ground at all.
But next spring from their coffins twain
Two lilies fair upgrew —
And by and by, o'er the roof-tree high,
They twined and they bloomed the whole year through.
How read you the riddle?

GUDMUND. [Looks searchingly at her.]

I scarce can say.

MARGIT.

You may doubtless read it in many a way;
But its truest meaning, methinks, is clear:
The church can never sever two that hold each other dear.

GUDMUND. [To himself.]

Ye saints, if she should — ? Lest worse befall,
'Tis time indeed I told her all!
   [Aloud.

Do you wish for my happiness — Margit, tell!

MARGIT. [In joyful agitation.]

Wish for it! I!

GUDMUND.

> Then, wot you well,
> The joy of my life now rests with you —

MARGIT. [With an outburst.]

Gudmund!

GUDMUND.

Listen! 'tis the time you knew —

[He stops suddenly.
[Voices and laughter are heard by the river bank. SIGNE and
other GIRLS enter from the right, accompanied by KNUT,
ERIK, and several YOUNGER MEN.

KNUT.

[Still at a distance.] Gudmund Alfson! Wait; I must speak a word
with you.

[He stops, talking to ERIK. The other GUESTS in the meantime
enter the house.

MARGIT.

[To herself.] The joy of his life —! What else can he mean
but —! [Half aloud.] Signe — my dear, dear sister!

[She puts her arm round SIGNE's waist, and they go towards
the back talking to each other.

GUDMUND.

[Softly as he follows them with his eyes.] Aye, so it were wisest. Both Signe and I must away from Solhoug. Knut Gesling has shown himself my friend; he will help me.

KNUT.

[Softly, to ERIK.] Yes, yes, I say, Gudmund is her kinsman; he can best plead my cause.

ERIK.

Well, as you will.

[He goes into the house.

KNUT.

[Approaching.] Listen, Gudmund —

GUDMUND.

[Smiling.] Come you to tell me that you dare no longer let me go free.

KNUT.

Dare! Be at your ease as to that. Knut Gesling dares whatever he will. No, 'tis another matter. You know that here in the district, I am held to be a wild, unruly companion —

GUDMUND.

Aye, and if rumour lies not —

KNUT.

Why no, much that it reports may be true enough. But now, I must tell you —

[They go, conversing, up towards the back.

SIGNE.

[To MARGIT, as they come forward beside the house.] I understand you not. You speak as though an unlooked-for happiness had befallen you. What is in your mind?

MARGIT.

Signe — you are still a child; you know not what it means to have ever in your heart the dread of — [Suddenly breaking off.] Think, Signe, what it must be to wither and die without ever having lived.

SIGNE.

[Looks at her in astonishment, and shakes her head.] Nay, but, Margit — ?

MARGIT.

Aye, aye, you do not understand, but none the less —

[They go up again, talking to each other. GUD-MUND and KNUT come down on the other side.

GUDMUND.

Well, if so it be — if this wild life no longer contents you — then I will give you the best counsel that ever friend gave to friend: take to wife an honourable maiden.

KNUT.

Say you so? And if I now told you that 'tis even that I have in mind?

GUDMUND.

Good luck and happiness to you then, Knut Gesling! And now you must know that I too—

KNUT.

You? Are you, too, so purposed?

GUDMUND.

Aye truly. But the King's wrath—I am a banished man—

KNUT.

Nay, to that you need give but little thought. As yet there is no one here, save Dame Margit, that knows aught of the matter; and so long as I am your friend, you have one in whom you can trust securely. Now I must tell you—

[He proceeds in a whisper as they go up again.

SIGNE.

[As she and MARGIT again advance.] But tell me then Margit—!

MARGIT.

More I dare not tell you.

SIGNE.

Then will I be more open-hearted than you. But first answer me one question. [Bashfully, with hesitation.] Is there no one who has told you anything concerning me?

MARGIT.

Concerning you? Nay, what should that be?

SIGNE.

[As before, looking downwards.] You said to me this morning: if a wooer came riding hither—?

MARGIT.

That is true. [To herself.] Knut Gesling—has he already—? [Eagerly to SIGNE.] Well? What then?

SIGNE.

[Softly, but with exultation.] The wooer has come! He has come, Margit! I knew not then whom you meant; but now—!

MARGIT.

And what have you answered him?

SIGNE.

Oh, how should I know? [Flinging her arms round her sister's neck.] But the world seems to me so rich and beautiful since the moment when he told me that he held me dear.

MARGIT.

Why, Signe, Signe, I cannot understand that you should so quickly—!
You scarce knew him before to-day.

SIGNE.

Oh, 'tis but little I yet know of love; but this I know that what
the song says is true:
Full swiftly 'tis sown; ere a moment speeds by,
Deep, deep in the heart love is rooted for aye—

MARGIT.

So be it; and since so it is, I need no longer hold aught concealed from you. Ah—

[She stops suddenly, as she sees KNUT and GUDMUND approaching.

KNUT.

[In a tone of satisfaction.] Ha, this is as I would have it,
Gudmund. Here is my hand!

MARGIT.

[To herself.] What is this?

GUDMUND.

[To KNUT.] And here is mine!

[They shake hands.

KNUT.

But now we must each of us name who it is —

GUDMUND.

Good. Here at Solhoug, among so many fair women, I have found her whom —

KNUT.

I too. And I will bear her home this very night, if it be needful.

MARGIT.

[Who has approached unobserved.] All saints in heaven!

GUDMUND.

[Nods to KNUT.] The same is my intent.

SIGNE.

[Who has also been listening.] Gudmund!

GUDMUND AND KNUT.

[Whispering to each other, as they both point at Signe.] There she is!

GUDMUND.

[Starting.] Aye, mine.

KNUT.

[Likewise.] No, mine!

MARGIT.

[Softly, half bewildered.] Signe!

GUDMUND.

[As before, to KNUT.] What mean you by that?

KNUT.

I mean that 'tis Signe whom I—

GUDMUND.

Signe! Signe is my betrothed in the sight of God.

MARGIT.

[With a cry.] It was she! No—no!

GUDMUND.

[To himself, as he catches sight of her.] Margit! She has heard everything.

KNUT.

Ho, ho! So this is how it stands? Nay, Dame Margit, 'tis needless to put on such an air of wonder; now I understand everything.

MARGIT.

[To SIGNE.] But not a moment ago you said—? [Suddenly grasping the situation.] 'Twas Gudmund you meant!

SIGNE.

[Astonished.] Yes, did you not know it! But what ails you, Margit?

MARGIT.

[In an almost toneless voice.] Nay, nothing, nothing.

KNUT.

[To MARGIT.] And this morning, when you made me give my word that I would stir no strife here to-night—you already knew that Gudmund Alfson was coming. Ha, ha, think not that you can hoodwink Knut Gesling! Signe has become dear to me. Even this morning 'twas but my hasty vow that drove me to seek her hand; but now—

SIGNE.

[To MARGIT.] He? Was this the wooer that was in your mind?

MARGIT.

Hush, hush!

KNUT.

[Firmly and harshly.] Dame Margit—you are her elder sister; you shall give me an answer.

MARGIT.

[Battling with herself.] Signe has already made her choice; —
I have naught to answer.

KNUT.

Good; then I have nothing more to do at Solhoug. But after midnight — mark you this — the day is at an end; then you may chance to
see me again, and then Fortune must decide whether it be Gudmund or I that shall bear Signe away from this house.

GUDMUND.

Aye, try if you dare; it shall cost you a bloody sconce.

SIGNE.

[In terror.] Gudmund! By all the saints — !

KNUT.

Gently, gently, Gudmund Alfson! Ere sunrise you shall be in my
power. And she — your lady-love — [Goes up to the door, beckons
and calls in a low voice.] Erik! Erik! come hither! we must away to
our kinsfolk. [Threateningly, while ERIK shows himself in the
doorway.] Woe upon you all when I come again!

[He and ERIK go off to the left at the back.

SIGNE.

[Softly to GUDMUND.] Oh, tell me, what does all this mean?

GUDMUND.

[Whispering.] We must both leave Solhoug this very night.

SIGNE.

God shield me — you would — !

GUDMUND.

Say nought of it! No word to any one, not even to your sister.

MARGIT.

[To herself.] She — it is she! She of whom he had scarce thought before to-night. Had I been free, I know well whom he had chosen. — Aye, free!

[BENGT and GUESTS, both Men and Women enter from the house.

YOUNG MEN AND MAIDENS.

Out here, out here be the feast arrayed,
While the birds are asleep in the greenwood shade,
How sweet to sport in the flowery glade
   'Neath the birches.

Out here, out here, shall be mirth and jest,
No sigh on the lips and no care in the breast,
When the fiddle is tuned at the dancers' 'hest,
   'Neath the birches.

BENGT.

That is well, that is well! So I fain would see it! I am merry, and my wife likewise; and therefore I pray ye all to be merry along with us.

ONE OF THE GUESTS.

Aye, now let us have a stave-match.*

*A contest in impromptu verse-making.

MANY.

[Shout.] Yes, yes, a stave-match!

ANOTHER GUEST.

Nay, let that be; it leads but to strife at the feast. [Lowering his voice.] Bear in mind that Knut Gesling is with us to-night.

SEVERAL.

[Whispering among themselves.] Aye, aye, that is true. Remember the last time, how he—. Best beware.

AN OLD MAN.

But you, Dame Margit—I know your kind had ever wealth of tales in store; and you yourself, even as a child, knew many a fair legend.

MARGIT.

Alas! I have forgot them all. But ask Gudmund Alfson, my kinsman; he knows a tale that is merry enough.

GUDMUND.

[In a low voice, imploringly.] Margit!

MARGIT.

Why, what a pitiful countenance you put on! Be merry, Gudmund! Be merry! Aye, aye, it comes easy to you, well I wot. [Laughing, to the GUESTS.] He has seen the huldra to-night. She would fain have tempted him; but Gudmund is a faithful swain. [Turns again to GUDMUND.] Aye, but the tale is not finished yet. When you bear away your lady-love, over hill and through forest, be sure you turn not round; be sure you never look back—the huldra sits laughing behind every bush; and when all is done— [In a low voice, coming close up to him.] —you will go no further than she will let you.

[She crosses to the right.

SIGNE.

Oh, God! Oh, God!

BENGT.

[Going around among the GUESTS in high contentment.] Ha, ha, ha! Dame Margit knows how to set the mirth afoot! When she takes it in hand, she does it much better than I.

GUDMUND.

[To himself.] She threatens! I must tear the last hope out of her breast; else will peace never come to her mind. [Turns to the GUESTS.] I mind me of a little song. If it please you to hear it—

SEVERAL OF THE GUESTS.

Thanks, thanks, Gudmund Alfson!

[They close around him some sitting, others standing. MARGIT leans against a tree in front on the right. SIGNE stands on the left, near the house.

GUDMUND.

I rode into the wildwood,
  I sailed across the sea,
But 'twas at home I wooed and won
  A maiden fair and free.

It was the Queen of Elfland,
  She waxed full wroth and grim:
Never, she swore, shall that maiden fair
  Ride to the church with him.

Hear me, thou Queen of Elfland,
  Vain, vain are threat and spell;
For naught can sunder two true hearts
  That love each other well!

AN OLD MAN.

That is a right fair song. See how the young swains cast their glances thitherward! [Pointing towards the GIRLS.] Aye, aye, doubtless each has his own.

BENGT.

[Making eyes at MARGIT.] Yes, I have mine, that is sure enough. Ha, ha, ha!

MARGIT.

[To herself, quivering.] To have to suffer all this shame and scorn! No, no; now to essay the last remedy.

BENGT.

What ails you? Meseems you look so pale.

MARGIT.

'Twill soon pass over. [Turns to the GUESTS.] Did I say e'en now that I had forgotten all my tales? I bethink me now that I remember one.

BENGT.

Good, good, my wife! Come, let us hear it.

YOUNG GIRLS.

[Urgently.] Yes, tell it us, tell it us, Dame Margit!

MARGIT.

I almost fear that 'twill little please you; but that must be as it may.

GUDMUND.

[To himself.] Saints in heaven, surely she would not—!

MARGIT.

It was a fair and noble maid,
She dwelt in her father's hall;
Both linen and silk did she broider and braid,
Yet found in it solace small.
For she sat there alone in cheerless state,
Empty were hall and bower;
In the pride of her heart, she was fain to mate
With a chieftain of pelf and power.

But now 'twas the Hill King, he rode from the north,
With his henchmen and his gold;
On the third day at night he in triumph fared forth,
Bearing her to his mountain hold.
Full many a summer she dwelt in the hill;
Out of beakers of gold she could drink at her will.
Oh, fair are the flowers of the valley, I trow,
But only in dreams can she gather them now!
'Twas a youth, right gentle and bold to boot,
Struck his harp with such magic might
That it rang to the mountain's inmost root,
Where she languished in the night.
The sound in her soul waked a wondrous mood —
Wide open the mountain-gates seemed to stand;
The peace of God lay over the land,
And she saw how it all was fair and good.
There happened what never had happened before;
She had wakened to life as his harp-strings thrilled;
And her eyes were opened to all the store
Of treasure wherewith the good earth is filled.
For mark this well: it hath ever been found
That those who in caverns deep lie bound
Are lightly freed by the harp's glad sound.
He saw her prisoned, he heard her wail —
But he cast unheeding his harp aside,
Hoisted straightway his silken sail,
And sped away o'er the waters wide
To stranger strands with his new-found bride.
    [With ever-increasing passion.

So fair was thy touch on the golden strings
That my breast heaves high and my spirit sings!
I must out, I must out to the sweet green leas!
I die in the Hill-King's fastnesses!
He mocks at my woe as he clasps his bride
And sails away o'er the waters wide.
    [Shrieks.

With me all is over; my hill-prison barred;
Unsunned is the day, and the night all unstarred.

[She totters and, fainting, seeks to support herself against
the trunk of a tree.

SIGNE.

[Weeping, has rushed up to her, and takes her in her arms.]
Margit! My sister!

GUDMUND.

[At the same time, supporting her.] Help! help! she is dying!

[BENGT and the GUESTS flock round them with cries of alarm.

ACT THIRD

The hall at Solhoug as before, but now in disorder after the feast.
  It is night still, but with a glimmer of approaching dawn in
  the room and over the landscape without.

BENGT stands outside in the passage-way, with a beaker of ale in
  his hand. A party of GUESTS are in the act of leaving the
  house. In the room a MAID-SERVANT is restoring order.

BENGT.

[Calls to the departing GUESTS.] God speed you, then, and bring
you back ere long to Solhoug. Methinks you, like the rest, might
have stayed and slept till morning. Well, well! Yet hold—I'll e'en go
with you to the gate. I must drink your healths once more.

[He goes out.

GUESTS. [Sing in the distance.]

Farewell, and God's blessing on one and all
  Beneath this roof abiding!
The road must be faced. To the fiddler we call:
  Tune up! Our cares deriding,
    With dance and with song
We'll shorten the way so weary and long.
  Right merrily off we go.

[The song dies away in the distance.
[MARGIT enters the hall by the door on the right.

MAID.

God save us, my lady, have you left your bed?

MARGIT.

I am well. Go you and sleep. Stay — tell me, are the guests all gone?

MAID.

No, not all; some wait till later in the day; ere now they are sleeping sound.

MARGIT.

And Gudmund Alfson — ?

MAID.

He, too, is doubtless asleep. [Points to the right.] 'Tis some time since he went to his chamber — yonder, across the passage.

MARGIT.

Good; you may go.

[The MAID goes out to the left.
[MARGIT walks slowly across the hall, seats herself by the table on the right, and gazes out at the open window.

MARGIT.

To-morrow, then, Gudmund will ride away
Out into the world so great and wide.

Alone with my husband here I must stay;
And well do I know what will then betide.
Like the broken branch and the trampled flower
I shall suffer and fade from hour to hour.
    [Short pause; she leans back in her chair.

I once heard a tale of a child blind from birth,
Whose childhood was full of joy and mirth;
For the mother, with spells of magic might,
Wove for the dark eyes a world of light.
And the child looked forth with wonder and glee
Upon the valley and hill, upon land and sea.
Then suddenly the witchcraft failed —
The child once more was in darkness pent;
Good-bye to games and merriment;
With longing vain the red cheeks paled.
And its wail of woe, as it pined away,
Was ceaseless, and sadder than words can say. —
Oh! like the child's my eyes were sealed,
To the light and the life of summer blind —
    [She springs up.

But now —! And I in this cage confined!
No, now is the worth of my youth revealed!
Three years of life I on him have spent —
My husband — but were I longer content
This hapless, hopeless weird to dree,
Meek as a dove I needs must be.
I am wearied to death of petty brawls;
The stirring life of the great world calls.
I will follow Gudmund with shield and bow,
I will share his joys, I will soothe his woe,
Watch o'er him both by night and day.
All that behold shall envy the life
Of the valiant knight and Margit his wife. —
His wife!
    [Wrings her hands.

Oh God, what is this I say!
Forgive me, forgive me, and oh! let me feel
The peace that hath power both to soothe and to heal.
   [Walks back and forward, brooding silently.

Signe, my sister — ? How hateful 'twere
To steal her glad young life from her!
But who can tell? In very sooth
She may love him but with the light love of youth.
   [Again silence; she takes out the little phial, looks long
     at it and says under her breath:

This phial — were I its powers to try —
My husband would sleep for ever and aye!
   [Horror-struck.

No, no! To the river's depths with it straight!
   [In the act of throwing it out of the window, stops.

And yet I could — 'tis not yet too late. —
   [With an expression of mingled horror and rapture, whispers.

With what a magic resistless might
Sin masters us in our own despite!
Doubly alluring methinks is the goal
I must reach through blood, with the wreck of my soul.

   [BENGT, with the empty beaker in his hand, comes in from
     the passageway; his face is red; he staggers slightly.

BENGT.

[Flinging the beaker upon the table on the left.] My faith, this has been a feast that will be the talk of the country. [Sees MARGIT.] Eh, are you there? You are well again. Good, good.

MARGIT.

[Who in the meantime has concealed the phial.] Is the door barred?

BENGT.

[Seating himself at the table on the left.] I have seen to everything. I went with the last guests as far as the gates. But what became of Knut Gesling to-night?—Give me mead, Margit! I am thirsty Fill this cup.

> [MARGIT fetches a flagon of the mead from a cupboard, and and fills the goblet which is on the table before him.

MARGIT.

[Crossing to the right with the flagon.] You asked about Knut Gesling.

BENGT.

That I did. The boaster, the braggart! I have not forgot his threats of yester-morning.

MARGIT.

He used worse words when he left to-night.

BENGT.

He did? So much the better. I will strike him dead.

MARGIT.

[Smiling contemptuously.] H'm —

BENGT.

I will kill him, I say! I fear not to face ten such fellows as he. In the store-house hangs my grandfather's axe; its shaft is inlaid with silver; with that axe in my hands, I tell you —! [Thumps the table and drinks.] To-morrow I shall arm myself, go forth with all my men, and slay Knut Gesling.

[Empties the beaker.

MARGIT.

[To herself.] Oh, to have to live with him!

[Is in the act of leaving the room.

BENGT.

Margit, come here! Fill my cup again. [She approaches; he tries to draw her down on his knee.] Ha, ha, ha! You are right fair, Margit! I love thee well!

MARGIT.

[Freeing herself.] Let me go!

[Crosses, with the goblet in her hand, to the left.

BENGT.

You are not in the humour to-night. Ha, ha, ha! That means no great matter, I know.

MARGIT.

[Softly, as she fills the goblet.] Oh, that this might be the last beaker I should fill for you.

[She leaves the goblet on the table and is making her way out to the left.

BENGT.

Hark to me, Margit. For one thing you may thank Heaven, and that is, that I made you my wife before Gudmund Alfson came back.

MARGIT.

Why so?

BENGT.

Why, say you? Am not I ten times the richer man? And certain I am that he would have sought you for his wife, had you not been the mistress of Solhoug.

MARGIT.

[Drawing nearer and glancing at the goblet.] Say you so?

BENGT.

I could take my oath upon it. Bengt Gauteson has two sharp eyes in his head. But he may still have Signe.

MARGIT.

And you think he will — ?

BENGT.

Take her? Aye, since he cannot have you. But had you been free, — then — Ha, ha, ha! Gudmund is like the rest. He envies me my wife. That is why I set such store by you, Margit. Here with the goblet again. And let it be full to the brim!

MARGIT.

[Goes unwillingly across to the right.] You shall have it straightway.

BENGT.

Knut Gesling is a suitor for Signe, too, but him I am resolved to slay. Gudmund is an honourable man; he shall have her. Think, Margit, what good days we shall have with them for neighbours. We will go a-visiting each other, and then will we sit the live-long day, each with his wife on his knee, drinking and talking of this and that.

MARGIT.

[Whose mental struggle is visibly becoming more severe, involuntarily takes out the phial as she says:] No doubt no doubt!

BENGT.

Ha, ha, ha! it may be that at first Gudmund will look askance at me when I take you in my arms; but that, I doubt not, he will soon get over.

MARGIT.

This is more than woman can bear! [Pours the contents of the phial into the goblet, goes to the window and throws out the phial, then says, without looking at him.] Your beaker is full.

BENGT.

Then bring it hither!

MARGIT.

[Battling in an agony of indecision, at last says.] I pray you drink no more to-night!

BENGT.

[Leans back in his chair and laughs.] Oho! You are impatient for my coming? Get you in; I will follow you soon.

MARGIT.

[Suddenly decided.] Your beaker is full. [Points.] There it is.

[She goes quickly out to the left.

BENGT.

[Rising.] I like her well. It repents me not a whit that I took her to wife, though of heritage she owned no more than yonder goblet and the brooches of her wedding gown.

[He goes to the table at the window and takes the goblet.
[A HOUSE-CARL enters hurriedly and with scared looks, from
  the back.

HOUSE-CARL.

[Calls.] Sir Bengt, Sir Bengt! haste forth with all the speed
you can! Knut Gesling with an armed train is drawing near
the house.

BENGT.

[Putting down the goblet.] Knut Gesling? Who brings the tidings?

HOUSE-CARL.

Some of your guests espied him on the road beneath, and
hastened back to warn you.

BENGT.

E'en so. Then will I —! Fetch me my grandfather's battle-axe!

[He and the HOUSE-CARL go out at the back.
[Soon after, GUDMUND and SIGNE enter quietly and cautiously
  by the door at the back.

SIGNE. [In muffled tones.]

It must then, be so!

GUDMUND. [Also softly.]

> Necessity's might
Constrains us.

SIGNE.

> Oh! thus under cover of night
To steal from the valley where I was born?
> [Dries her eyes.

Yet shalt thou hear no plaint forlorn.
'Tis for thy sake my home I flee;
Wert thou not outlawed, Gudmund dear,
I'd stay with my sister.

GUDMUND.

> Only to be
Ta'en by Knut Gesling, with bow and spear,
Swung on the croup of his battle-horse,
And made his wife by force.

SIGNE.

> Quick, let us flee. But whither go?

GUDMUND.

Down by the fiord a friend I know;
He'll find us a ship. O'er the salt sea foam
We'll sail away south to Denmark's bowers.
There waits you there a happy home;
Right joyously will fleet the hours;
The fairest of flowers they bloom in the shade

Of the beech-tree glade.

SIGNE. [Bursts into tears.]

Farewell, my poor sister! Like my mother tender
Thou hast guarded the ways my feet have trod,
Hast guided my footsteps, aye praying to God,
The Almighty, to be my defender. —
Gudmund — here is a goblet filled with mead;
Let us drink to her; let us wish that ere long
Her soul may again be calm and strong,
And that God may be good to her need.

[She takes the goblet into her hands.

GUDMUND.

Aye, let us drain it, naming her name!
　[Starts.

Stop!
　[Takes the goblet from her.

For meseems it is the same —

SIGNE.

'Tis Margit's beaker.

GUDMUND. [Examining it carefully.]

　By Heaven, 'tis so!
I mind me still of the red wine's glow
As she drank from it on the day we parted

To our meeting again in health and glad-hearted.
To herself that draught betided woe.
No, Signe, ne'er drink wine or mead
From that goblet.
 [Pours its contents out at the window.

We must away with all speed.

[Tumult and calls without, at the back.

SIGNE.

List, Gudmund! Voices and trampling feet!

GUDMUND.

Knut Gesling's voice!

SIGNE.

O save us, Lord!

GUDMUND. [Places himself in front of her.]

Nay, nay, fear nothing, Signe sweet —
I am here, and my good sword.

[MARGIT comes in in haste from the left.

MARGIT.

[Listening to the noise.] What means this? Is my husband — ?

GUDMUND AND SIGNE.

Margit!

MARGIT.

[Catches sight of them.] Gudmund! And Signe! Are you here?

SIGNE.

[Going towards her.] Margit — dear sister!

MARGIT.

[Appalled, having seen the goblet which GUDMUND still holds in his hand.] The goblet! Who has drunk from it?

GUDMUND.

[Confused.] Drunk —? I and Signe — we meant —

MARGIT.

[Screams.] O God, have mercy! Help! Help! They will die!

GUDMUND.

[Setting down the goblet.] Margit —!

SIGNE.

What ails you, sister?

MARGIT.

[Towards the back.] Help, help! Will no one help?

[A HOUSE-CARL rushes in from the passage-way.

HOUSE-CARL.

[Calls in a terrified voice.] Lady Margit! Your husband —!

MARGIT.

He — has he, too, drunk —!

GUDMUND.

[To himself.] Ah! now I understand —

HOUSE-CARL.

Knut Gesling has slain him.

SIGNE.

Slain!

GUDMUND.

[Drawing his sword.] Not yet, I hope. [Whispers to MARGIT.] Fear not. No one has drunk from your goblet.

MARGIT.

Then thanks be to God, who has saved us all!

> [She sinks down on a chair to the left. Gudmund hastens towards the door at the back.

ANOTHER HOUSE-CARL.

[Enters, stopping him.] You come too late. Sir Bengt is dead.

GUDMUND.

Too late, then, too late.

HOUSE-CARL.

The guests and your men have prevailed against the murderous crew. Knut Gesling and his men are prisoners. Here they come.

> [GUDMUND's men, and a number of GUESTS and HOUSE-CARLS, lead in KNUT GESLING, ERIK OF HEGGE, and several of KNUT's men, bound.

KNUT.

> [Who is pale, says in a low voice.] Man-slayer, Gudmund. What say you to that?

GUDMUND.

Knut, Knut, what have you done?

ERIK.

'Twas a mischance, of that I can take my oath.

KNUT.

> He ran at me swinging his axe; I meant but to defend myself, and struck the death-blow unawares.

ERIK.

Many here saw all that befell.

KNUT.

Lady Margit, crave what fine you will. I am ready to pay it.

MARGIT.

I crave naught. God will judge us all. Yet stay — one thing I require. Forgo your evil design upon my sister.

KNUT.

Never again shall I essay to redeem my baleful pledge. From this day onward I am a better man. Yet would I fain escape dishonourable punishment for my deed. [To GUDMUND.] Should you be restored to favour and place again, say a good word for me to the King!

GUDMUND.

I? Ere the sun sets, I must have left the country.

> [Astonishment amongst the GUESTS. ERIK in whispers, explains the situation.

MARGIT.

[To GUDMUND.] You go? And Signe with you?

SIGNE.

[Beseechingly.] Margit!

MARGIT.

Good fortune follow you both!

SIGNE.

[Flinging her arms round MARGIT's neck.] Dear sister!

GUDMUND.

Margit, I thank you. And now farewell. [Listening.] Hush!
I hear the tramp of hoofs in the court-yard.

SIGNE.

[Apprehensively.] Strangers have arrived.

[A HOUSE-CARL appears in the doorway at the back.

HOUSE-CARL.

The King's men are without. They seek Gudmund Alfson.

SIGNE.

Oh God!

MARGIT.

[In great alarm.] The King's men!

GUDMUND.

All is at an end, then. Oh Signe, to lose you now — could
there be a harder fate?

KNUT.

Nay, Gudmund; sell your life dearly, man! Unbind us; we
are ready to fight for you, one and all.

ERIK.

[Looks out.] 'Twould be in vain; they are too many for us.

SIGNE.

Here they come. Oh Gudmund, Gudmund!

[The KING's MESSENGER enters from the back, with his escort.

MESSENGER.

In the King's name I seek you, Gudmund Alfson, and bring you his behests.

GUDMUND.

Be it so. Yet am I guiltless; I swear it by all that is holy!

MESSENGER.

We know it.

GUDMUND.

What say you?

[Agitation amongst those present.

MESSENGER.

I am ordered to bid you as a guest to the King's house. His friendship is yours as it was before, and along with it he bestows on you rich fiefs.

GUDMUND.

Signe!

SIGNE.

Gudmund!

GUDMUND.

But tell me—?

MESSENGER.

Your enemy, the Chancellor Audun Hugleikson, has fallen.

GUDMUND.

The Chancellor!

GUESTS.

[To each other, in half-whisper.] Fallen!

MESSENGER.

Three days ago he was beheaded at Bergen. [Lowering his voice.]
His offence was against Norway's Queen.

MARGIT. [Placing herself between GUDMUND and SIGNE.]

Thus punishment treads on the heels of crime!
Protecting angels, loving and bright,
Have looked down in mercy on me to-night,
And come to my rescue while yet it was time.
Now know I that life's most precious treasure
Is nor worldly wealth nor earthly pleasure,
I have felt the remorse, the terror I know,
Of those who wantonly peril their soul,
To St. Sunniva's cloister forthwith I go. —

[Before GUDMUND and SIGNE can speak.

Nay: think not to move me or control.
    [Places SIGNE's hand in GUDMUND's.

Take her then Gudmund, and make her your bride.
Your union is holy; God's on your side.

            [Waving farewell, she goes towards the doorway
            on the left. GUDMUND and SIGNE follow her, she
            stops them with a motion of her hand, goes out,
            and shuts the door behind her. At this moment the
            sun rises and sheds its light in the hall.

GUDMUND.

Signe — my wife! See, the morning glow!
'Tis the morning of our young love. Rejoice!

SIGNE.

All my fairest of dreams and of memories I owe
To the strains of thy harp and the sound of thy voice.
My noble minstrel, to joy or sadness
Tune thou that harp as seems thee best;
There are chords, believe me, within my breast
To answer to thine, or of woe or of gladness.

CHORUS OF MEN AND WOMEN.

Over the earth keeps watch the eye of light,
Guardeth lovingly the good man's ways,
Sheddeth round him its consoling rays; —

Praise be to the Lord in heaven's height!

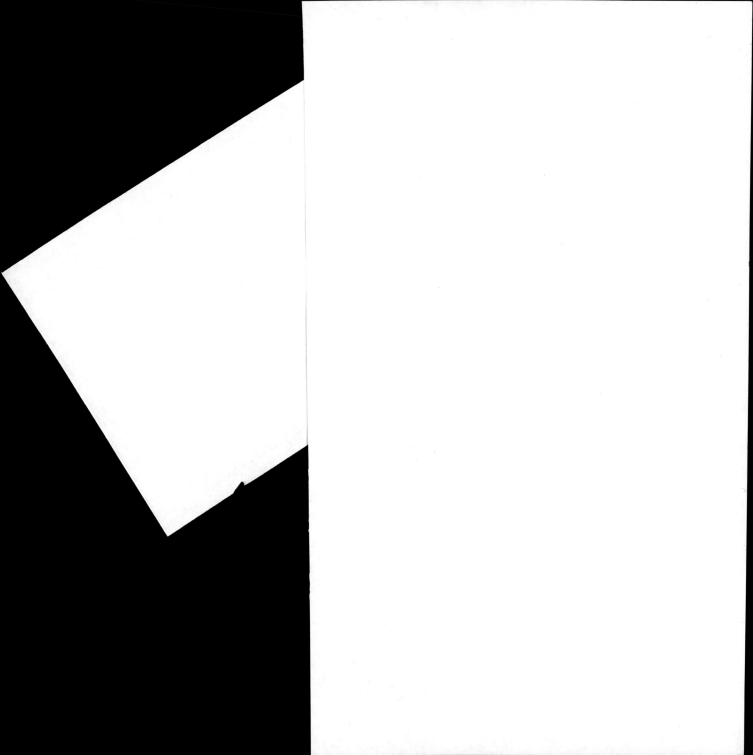

0 1341 1463956 7

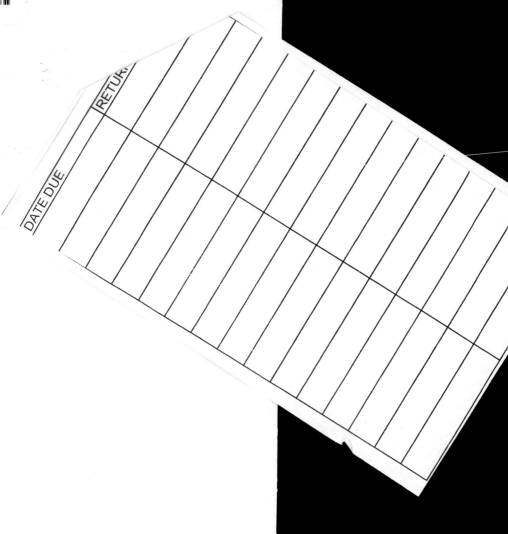

DATE DUE | RETUR

CPSIA information can be obtained at www.ICGtesting.com
Printed in the USA
LVOW101810210613

339670LV00005B/26/P

9 783842 486935

Australian Wildflowers in Colour

Poached Egg Daisies, *Myriocephalus stuartii*, text: page 94

AUSTRALIAN WILDFLOWERS in COLOUR

Photographs
DOUGLASS BAGLIN

Text
BARBARA MULLINS

REED

First published 1969
Reprinted 1974, 1977, 1979
This revised edition 1985
Reprinted 1988

REED BOOKS PTY LTD
2 Aquatic Drive, Frenchs Forest, NSW 2086.

National Library of Australia
Cataloguing in Publication data
Mullins, Barbara G.
    Australian wildflowers in colour.

    (Reed colourbook series).
    Index.
    Bibliography.
    ISBN 0 7301 0079 0.

    1. Wild flowers — Australia. I. Baglin,
    Douglass, photographer. II. Title. (Series).
582.130994

Typeset in Australia by Post Typesetters, Brisbane.
Printed in Singapore for Imago Productions (F.E.) Pte. Ltd.

CONTENTS

INTRODUCTION

AUSTRALIA, island isolated by sea and time, continent encompassing tropical rain forests and inland desert, alpine plateaux and salty sand-dunes, has the most diverse and varied flora in the world. The number of different species has been estimated to be about 20,000 to 25,000, the majority of them found nowhere else. Many are still undiscovered.

In the rain forests of Queensland are trees not yet described, though the area is known to contain plants with valuable medicinal properties as well as of great beauty. Sandy heathlands and stony deserts have produced native plants which have learned to cope with harsh environments or perish; four thousand million years of natural selection have found a myriad answers to drought and heat which may well solve problems of survival and sustain the life of mankind. The south-west corner of Western Australia, isolated by sea and desert for countless aeons and probably the most ancient undisturbed land mass on the face of the earth, has developed a remarkably individual and specialised flora. The Hawkesbury sandstone country of coastal New South Wales contains a greater variety of plants than the whole of the British Isles; many are confined to this limited area, which includes the populous and growing cities of Sydney, Newcastle and Wollongong.

Australia's flora is in danger: threatened by rutile mining on the coast and the exploitation of other mineral deposits inland, by urban and rural development. Its wealth is not yet known, and, unlike our mineral resources, it is a treasure which can be used again and again — provided we do not destroy it.

The first person to report on Australia's remarkable flora was William Dampier, adventurer and buccaneer, who collected specimens of Australian plants when he visited the north-west coast in 1688 and 1699. These specimens, still preserved in the British Museum and at Oxford, included the flamboyant Sturt's Desert Pea which early botanist Allan Cunningham called *Clianthus dampieri* in his honour (a name later superseded by *Clianthus formosus*) and a species of *Dampiera*, the genus which now commemorates him.

Little interest was aroused, however, until almost a century later. In the autumn of 1770, Joseph Banks and Dr. Solander, botanists with Captain James Cook's expedition, collected the first specimens from the east coast. They were amazed at the profusion of species hitherto unknown. Cook recorded: "The great quantity of plants Mr. Banks and Dr. Solander found in this place occasioned my giving it the name of Botany Bay." Years later, Banks, speaking of the "many usefull and beautifull Plants with which the Country in the neighbourhood of Jacksons' Bay is known to abound," urged that a ship sailing to the settlement there "be fitted for the reception of pots" with the object of bringing back specimens for His Majesty's Botanic Garden of Kew.

Next to add to knowledge of Australia's flora was Jacques-Julien Labillardière, botanist with Bruny D'Entrecasteaux's expedition in search of the lost La Perouse. In 1792, with "an industry all but indefatigable" (to quote Sir Joseph Banks) he collected specimens from Tasmania and Western Australia. On the homeward journey the ship, together with Labillardiere and his collection was seized by a British cruiser. It was at first proposed that the collection be added to the Royal Herbarium, and Banks was asked to examine the specimens and make a suitable selection. However

Banks successfully urged, "for the honour of the British nation and for the advancement of science", that "the right of captors to the collection should on this occasion be waived and that the whole should be returned to M. doctor Billardière ..." The genus *Billardiera* commemorates the name of the French naturalist. A compatriot whose name is also recorded in the flora of Australia is Leschenault de la Tour, botanist with Baudin's French scientific expedition of 1802 (*Lechenaultia*).

Perhaps the most significant contribution to early botanical knowledge in Australia was made by Robert Brown, a young Scottish botanist who accompanied Flinders in *Investigator* during 1801-2. Over a period of three and a half years Brown collected and described almost 4,000 species, the majority of them new to science. His great work, *Prodromus Florae Novae Hollandiae* is generally regarded as the foundation stone of systematic botany in Australia.

After Brown came other eminent scientists, each adding to the store of knowledge. Prominent among them were Allan Cunningham, botanist with Oxley's first expedition, most of whose collections are still preserved at the Royal Botanic Gardens, Kew; Baron Ferdinand von Mueller, whose long career of exploration, collection, and study of Australian plants, together with many published works, make him perhaps the most distinguished of all Australian botanists; and J. H. Maiden, responsible for much pioneer work on eucalypts and acacias.

Though the divergences in Australia's flora have long fascinated botanists, the affinities with the flora of the rest of the world are no less remarkable. The majority of Australian native species and indeed genera are endemic. In the main, however, the major plant families of other continents are also the principal plant families of Australia. Australia's flora is part of the world's flora, developed under conditions of isolation: its differences and resemblances merely underline this fact.

In this book, thirty-two families and over one hundred species have been illustrated; many more have been described. But since this constitutes less than one per cent of the total number of Australia's flowering plants, it is inevitable that many species — unique, popular, scientifically important, flamboyantly beautiful — have of necessity been omitted. Within the limitation of format we have endeavoured to present a broad pictorial record — to include little-known species from remote areas where the tourist seldom penetrates as well as popular garden favourites; to give a selection of the main groups of Australian flowers and a geographical cover of the Australian continent; to show plants of scientific interest and ornamental plants which have yet to grace the gardens of the world; and to emphasise the similarities and the differences. In short, to give a glimpse of the scope and contradictions of Australia's flora.

Plants have been arranged in families, according to the order in J. Hutchinson's *The Families of Flowering Plants*, second edition Vols. 1 and 2 (1959).

BARBARA MULLINS   DOUGLASS BAGLIN

GLOSSARY

anther: the part of the stamen which contains pollen.

auricle: ear-shaped lobe at base of leaf, petal, or other organ.

axil: angle formed by leaf and branch.

axis: stem or central part.

berry: fleshy fruit with seeds immersed in pulp.

bisexual: having both male and female parts in the same flower.

bipinnate: leaves twice divided in a pinnate manner.

bract: modified leaf associated with a flower or inflorescence, often small and scale-like.

calyx: (plural, calyces): the sepals collectively; the outer whorl of floral leaves.

capsule: dry fruit of 2 or more united carpels, which opens when ripe.

carpel: the female organ of the flower, composed of ovary, style, and stigma.

compound flowerhead: an inflorescence composed of a number of heads.

compound leaf: a leaf with 2 or more leaflets.

corolla: the petals collectively; the inner whorl of floral leaves.

cyme: an inflorescence with the oldest flowers towards the centre, often with each branch ending in a flower and younger flowers arising at lower branches.

drupe: a succulent fruit with a hard stone.

endemic: confined to a particular geographical region and found nowhere else.

ephemeral: short-lived: similar to an annual but occurring after rains in arid regions.

epiphyte: plant which grows on another but is not parasitic.

filament: stalk of the stamen.

follicle: dry, one-seeded fruit formed from a single pistil which splits open when ripe.

fruit: seed-bearing structure consisting of mature ovary and any additional parts of the flower which may remain attached to it.

genus (plural, genera): a group in biological classification, consisting of one or more species with a number of essential characteristics in common.

herb: a plant which does not produce a woody stem.

indusium: in Goodeniaceae, the pollen cup; in ferns, a covering over the sorus.

inferior ovary: ovary situated below the sepals and petals.

inflorescence: the disposition of the flowers on the floral axis.

involucral bracts: a whorl of bracts below or around the inflorescence.

lignotuber: a woody swelling at the base of a stem, which stores food and has dormant buds.

ligulate: strap-shaped.

linear: long, narrow, with parallel sides.

monotypic: having only one member, e.g. a genus with only one species.

nut: dry, one-seeded fruit which does not split open when mature.

operculum: cap of fused petals or perianth segments covering a flower bud; or the lid of a capsule which opens by a circular split.

ovary: the basal part of the pistil or female organ, in which the seeds develop.

palmate leaf: divided into leaflets, the leaflets diverging from a central point.

panicle: much-branched inflorescence, each stem with the youngest flowers toward the top.

pappus: modified sepals in many Asteraceae, which persists as an appendage of hairs, bristles or scales on the fruit.

perianth: calyx (sepals) and corolla (petals) collectively.

phyllodes: flattened leaf stalks which are leaflike and perform the function of leaves.

pinnate: compound leaf with leaflets arranged on each side of a common stalk; featherlike.

pistil: the female part of a flower, usually consisting of ovary, style, and stigma.

raceme: inflorescence of stalked flowers, with youngest flowers nearest the apex.

schizocarp: dry fruit which when ripe divides into several one-seeded carpels.

sclerophyll: plants with hard, stiff foliage.

sepals: the outer whorl of the flower, usually green; known collectively as calyx.

species: a group in biological classification, consisting of plants possessing distinctive characteristics in common and potentially capable of interbreeding to produce fertile offspring.

spike: inflorescence of stalkless flowers, the youngest flowers nearest the apex.

stamen: male part of the flowers, consisting of filament and anther.

stigma: that part of the female organ of the flower adapted for the reception of pollen.

stipules: pair of small appendages at the base of a leaf-insertion in certain plants.

style: that part of the female organ of the flower situated above the ovary and bearing the stigma.

superior ovary: ovary situated above the calyx.

tepals: individual perianth segments, particularly where corolla and calyx are not clearly differentiated.

terrestrial: growing in the ground.

trifoliolate: having 3 leaflets.

umbel: an inflorescence with all flower-stalks arising from a common point, often flat-topped with the flowers at the same level.

unisexual: either male or female: a flower with stamens or pistils but not both.

valvate: with edges touching.

ACKNOWLEDGEMENTS

The authors wish to extend their sincere thanks to the Director and staff of the National Herbarium of New South Wales, Royal Botanic Gardens, Sydney, for help in the identification of photographs and permission to use the research facilities of the National Herbarium Library. Particular thanks are extended to Dr. Mary Tindale, Miss Neridah Ford, Dr. Barbara Briggs, Mr. L. A. S. Johnson, and Mr. D. McGillivary for advice, helpful criticism, and endless patience in the face of many queries.

Also acknowledged with gratitude is the part played by Mr. Peter Baillieu of King Ranch Pty. Ltd., Mr. Tom Watson of Aerial Agriculture Pty. Ltd., Mr. Leo Corbett of Pitchi Richi, Mr. Walter Allwright of Alice Springs, and others whose cooperation made it possible to reach many remote and isolated areas and to present this broad geographical cover of the Australian continent.

FAMILY MIMOSACEAE

THE WATTLES

THE WATTLE family consists of about 40 genera and over 2,500 species of shrubs and trees, widely dispersed in tropical, subtropical, and temperate parts of the world, particularly Africa, South America, and Australia.

Because the fruit is usually a legume (true pod) this group of plants was originally classified with the cassias and the peas under the family Leguminosae. Nowadays this large and rather unwieldy family is usually divided into the Mimosaceae, the Fabaceae (formerly Papilionaceae), and the Caesalpiniaceae.

The family name comes from the genus *Mimosa*, so named because the leaves of many species "mimic" animal movements, drooping and closing at the touch of a finger, responding to darkness and light: the "sensitive plants" of European hothouses.

Australia has no true mimosas; here the family is represented mainly by acacias — wattles — though there are a half-dozen endemic species of the closely related *Albizia*, and a few of *Neptunia* (*Neptunia gracilis* is known as the native sensitive plant).

There are however over 650 indigenous *Acacia* species, all but a few of them confined to Australia. They form the largest genus in the flora of this land: they are the most widespread of all Australian plants. Great areas of country bear their names — mulga and brigalow, myall and gidgee. They inhabit places where even the eucalypt does not maintain an existence, blooming in profusion and brilliance in the sun-parched interior.

A wattle is Australia's national floral emblem; a wattle is featured on the coat-of-arms and coinage. The glorious gold of wattle against the blue of Australian skies is a national hallmark. But acacias are not confined to Australia; the genus also occurs in Africa, South and Central America, Asia, and the Pacific Islands. Gum arabic comes from an acacia of tropical Africa, catechu from an East Indian species; the Biblical shittah tree is an acacia. Indeed, the genus owes its name to Egyptian species known since ancient times as "akakia" (from the Greek *ake*, a point, a reference to the sharp stipules found on many African species).

Individual *Acacia* flowers, always very small, are massed together in globular heads or cylindrical spikes. These tightly packed flowers can be seen quite clearly in the buds, as shown in the illustration of *A. cynanophylla*, (plate 1, opposite) and the number present is often a guide to identification of a particular specimen. Once open, the numerous prominent stamens obscure the tiny petals, forming the fluffy golden balls and catkins we know as wattle blossom.

continues on page 12

Plate 1.

WESTERN AUSTRALIAN GOLDEN WATTLE —
Acacia cynanophylla

This highly ornamental wattle is a native of the south-western corner of the continent. It is a shrub or small tree, 3–8 m high, widely cultivated in gardens and now naturalised elsewhere in Australia. Deep yellow flowerballs are borne profusely in spring. Phyllodes are sickle-shaped and up to 15 cm long.

1

True leaves are always bipinnate (fernlike) but in most Australian wattles this compound structure is reduced to flattened stalks (known botanically as phyllodes) which perform the function of leaves.

These leaflike modified stalks are tougher than true leaves, and appear better able to withstand the arid conditions of many parts of Australia. They occur in an infinite variety of shapes and sizes: stiff and spinelike, long and narrow or reduced to mere prickles; broad, sickle-shaped, or hooked and bony; round, soft, and silvery. Some resemble pine-needles, others mimic red-tipped gum-leaves. All phyllodinous wattles, however, have this factor in common: seedling leaves are always bipinnate.

As the plants develop, the true leaves are reduced to phyllodes, and it is not uncommon, in young plants, to see the phyllode developing at the base of the compound leaf, or to find both phyllodes and bipinnate leaves on a plant that has been pruned or damaged. The majority of Australian wattles are phyllodinous; with the exception of a few species in the Pacific Islands and New Guinea this unique modification is confined to Australia.

continues on page 14

Plate 2.

COOTAMUNDRA WATTLE — *Acacia baileyana*

The spectacular Cootamundra wattle, widely cultivated both in Australia and overseas and probably the best-known of all acacias, was in nature confined to a very limited area on the south-western slopes of New South Wales. J. H. Maiden, the eminent botanist responsible for much pioneering work on Australian acacias, described it as "one of the most local of all wattles, being naturally found only in a small part of New South Wales — about Cootamundra, Bethungra, Big

Mimosa Run in the Wagga district, and thereabouts." Maiden added: "Ironically enough, this exclusively New South Wales wattle was named and described in a Victorian publication after a distinguished Queensland botanist — a sort of botanical federation, in fact." (It was named by the celebrated Victorian botanist Baron Ferdinand von Mueller in honour of the Queensland botanist F. M. Bailey.)

A. baileyana is one of the minority of Australian wattles which retain in maturity the feathery leaves of the seedling stage. It belongs to the Botryocephaleae, an exclusively Australian group of acacias with bipinnate leaves. A graceful, shapely tree, with soft, silvery-grey foliage, it ranges in height from 3–10 m and is laden with panicles of bright golden flowerheads in late winter and spring.

Plate 3.

PRICKLY MOSES — *Acacia echinula*

This is one of several wattles known by the vernacular name, Prickly Moses — the "Moses" being a corruption of mimosa, and not a reference to the Biblical hero, though the numerous, bright-yellow flowerballs of this species would appear to justify reference to his "burning bush". A wiry, erect shrub up to 2 m high, *A. echinula* flourishes on dry exposed ridges of the east coast and tablelands of New South Wales. Leaves are reduced to small, rigid phyllodes, shorter than the flowerheads and little more than prickles. It flowers in late winter and spring.

Plate 4.

SYDNEY GOLDEN WATTLE — *Acacia longifolia*

The Sydney Golden Wattle belongs to a group of acacias known botanically as the Juliflorae. These are phyllodinous wattles in which the individual flowers are massed into cylindrical or oblong spikes, rather than the more-familiar round flowerballs. A very hardy wattle, common in sandstone areas of eastern and southern Australia, it varies in size from a low shrub to a small tree. Long golden rods of sweet-scented flowers are borne in early spring.

12

2

3

4

The common name wattle, so widely applied to Australian acacias, is a relic of our first settlers. Derived from the Old English, *watul*, a hurdle, it is a term applied since Anglo-Saxon times to any flexible twigs interwoven to form a shelter. Early colonists used the pliant stems of acacia saplings to construct walls, sealing them with wet clay — the traditional "wattle and daub" huts of the pioneers.

Some Australian wattles have highly descriptive vernacular names. Two prickly species, *Acacia colletioides* and *A. tetragonophylla*, are known respectively as "Wait-a-while" and "Dead Finish". *A. acuminata* is commonly called "Raspberry Jam Tree" because the dark-red, closely grained timber smells strongly of raspberries when freshly cut. In many cases Aboriginal names have been retained — Wallowa, Cooba, Boree, Eumung and Yarran.

Wattles are prized mainly for their ornamental value. They vary in height from dwarf shrubs to tall forest trees. Flowers, often sweetly scented, range in colour from pale cream to deep orange; the flowering season extends throughout the whole year.

Though not usually long-lived, they are fast-growing. Many are extremely hardy, some species flourishing in sand-dunes exposed to salt spray, some in swamplands, and others on dry and stony ridges. Their rapid growth and ability to withstand harsh conditions make them useful for windbreaks and erosion control.

Some Australian acacias are valuable timber trees. The Blackwood (*A. melanoxylon*), which grows 20–30 m in rich coastal forests, is the source of an attractive figured cabinet wood. Mulga (*A. aneura*), a small shrubby tree of vast areas of the arid inland, produces an extremely hard timber of contrasting dark brown and golden yellow, which takes a high polish and is used for ornamental woodwork and curios. Aborigines used it for their narrow shields ("mulgas"). The timber of the Brigalow (*A. harpophylla*) is hard, heavy, and elastic, valuable for turners' work and extremely durable for fenceposts and similar purposes; it was also used by the Aborigines, notably for spears.

Perfumery oil is extracted commercially from *A. farnesiana*, (which grows in tropical regions of all five continents). Australian wattles such as *A. pycnantha* (pictured opposite), *A. decurrens* and *A. mearnsii* are rated as the world's best tan barks and are extensively cultivated overseas for this purpose.

Plate 5.

AUSTRALIAN GOLDEN WATTLE — *Acacia pycnantha*

This is the wattle featured on the national coat-of-arms and accepted as the floral emblem of Australia. A small tree, 4–8 m in height, it occurs naturally in South Australia, Victoria, and south-west New South Wales, but is extensively cultivated elsewhere. Masses of large, fragrant, deep-yellow flowerballs are borne in spring. Phyllodes are sickle-shaped, 8–15 cm long.
One of the hardiest of wattles, it thrives in sand and shallow soil, and is extremely drought-resistant, though somewhat frost-sensitive when young. It is commercially valuable as a source of tannin.

FAMILY FABACEAE
(formerly Papilionaceae)
THE BUTTERFLY PEAS

THIS FAMILY is known as the butterfly peas, a reference to the graceful winged flowers which characterise its members.

The pea family is a large one, widespread throughout the world and well represented in Australia by over 100 genera. Fruit is usually a legume, and, with the Mimosaceae and the Caesalpiniaceae, the family was originally grouped under the family Leguminosae. It includes herbs, shrubs, climbers, and trees.

Flowers always have 5 petals. The upper one, erect, usually large, is called the standard; it overlaps the others and encloses them in bud. The two lateral (side) petals form the characteristic butterfly wings, and the two lower ones are united into a wedgelike keel.

The standard varies in shape and size. In *Clianthus* (Sturt's Desert Pea) it is large, elongated and pointed. In *Oxylobium* (Native Holly), *Aotus* (Eggs-and-Bacon), and *Pultenaea* (Bush Peas) it is rounded.

Another distinguishing factor is the stamens. Always 10 in number, they are either free, all united into a tube, or 9 united and one free.

continues on page 18

Plate 6.

STURT'S DESERT PEA — *Clianthus formosus*

Sturt's Desert Pea, with its vivid red petals and glossy black central boss, is one of the most spectacular of all Australian native plants. It occurs naturally in the arid inland extending from Kalgoorlie to the Kimberleys, the off-shore islands of the Dampier Archipelago, and across the continent to the western plains of Queensland and New South Wales. The first specimens were gathered on the north-west coast by Dampier in 1699. It owes its common name to the explorer Charles Sturt, who collected samples near Broken Hill, New South Wales, during his journey to Cooper Creek in 1844. It is the official floral emblem for the State of South Australia.

Individual blooms, up to 10 cm long, hang in clusters at the top of short, erect stems. Stamens are united into a tube, with the exception of the upper one, which is free. Foliage is silky, and silvery-grey in colour. There are two forms: one, common in the Kalgoorlie region, is a prostrate runner with stems lying on the ground and covering several square metres from a single plant; the other, confined in nature to the Hamersley Range/Port Hedland district of Western Australia, is semi-erect. The latter form is the one more commonly cultivated in gardens.

The generic name, *Clianthus*, is aptly chosen, because it is from the Greek *kleos*, glory, and *anthos*, flower. There are only two species in the genus: Sturt's Desert Pea, confined to Australia, and the Red Kowhai or Parrot's Beak (*C. puniceus*), a highly ornamental small shrub native to New Zealand.

Plate 7.

NATIVE HOLLY — *Oxylobium ilicifolium*

The common name refers to dark green, holly-like leaves, deeply lobed and sharply pointed. Flowers are bright yellow, touched with red in the centre. It is a native of the east coast and mountains of Queensland, New South Wales and Victoria, an erect shrub, varying in height from 1–3 m.

Plate 8.

EGGS AND BACON — *Aotus ericoides*

This is one of several yellow and red native peas popularly known as "Eggs-and-Bacon"; an intriguing name but rather confusing since it is so widely applied. *A. ericoides* is a small shrub found in coastal and tableland areas of eastern states. Dainty yellow and red flowers are borne profusely in spring, almost obscuring the narrow dark green leaves.

6

7

8

Leaves may be simple or compound, often trifoliolate (simple leaves in threes on the one stem) or pinnate (compound leaves with leaflets arranged on opposite sides of a common leafstalk). In some species leaves end in a tendril.

The Pea family is a valuable one economically. It includes vegetables such as peas and beans, and fodder crops such as lucerne. Liquorice is obtained from the root of an Asiatic species of *Glycorrhiza*; Australia has one indigenous species. Indigo, the dye of commerce, is obtained from *Indigofera;* there are 20 to 25 indigenous species. The family also embraces many valuable timber trees, including the Australian Black Bean, *Castanospermum australe* (pictured on page 21). Peanuts belong to the Fabaceae, as do many lovely garden plants — lupin, broom, sweet pea, and wistaria.

The largest Australian genus is *Pultenaea*, with over 100 species. These are the Bush Peas, a group entirely confined to Australia, well represented in every State and particularly profuse in the Hawkesbury sandstone area of New South Wales. Bush peas can be found growing in coastal sand-dunes and on high mountains, in peaty swamps and on arid inland plains. They vary in habit from prostrate matlike plants to large shrubs.

Flowers are enclosed in brown, papery bracts. Usually yellow to orange-red (an exception is the pink-flowered *Pultenaea subalpina*), they are often massed at the end of branches into crowded heads, and the characteristic bracts can usually be seen between the individual flowers. Stamens are free. Leaves are small, simple, and alternate. The pod is small, egg-shaped, and often slightly inflated. It contains two seeds.

Other large, wholly Australian genera are *Daviesia* (about 70 species) commonly known as Bitter Peas, *Bossiaea* (about 40 to 50 species) and

Oxylobium, the Shaggy Peas, so-called because pods are often hairy. There are about 40 species in this last-named genus, all shrubs, ranging in habit from prostrate and wiry to tall and rigid. Flowers are yellow or orange, with a red keel. Stamens are free. This genus is represented in all States; it includes the Holly Pea (*Oxylobium ilicifolium*) pictured on page 17.

The genus *Chorizema* consists of 18 species, all except one confined to Western Australia. It was first described by botanist Labillardière who, as a member of Bruny D'Entrecasteaux's expedition in 1792, collected the first specimens near Esperance Bay. It is said that the delightful generic name (from *choros,* dance, and *zema*, drink) was chosen because he and his party danced for joy when they found the plant growing beside a waterhole; they had been for some time without water.

continues on page 20

Plate 9.

BUSH PEA — *Pultenaea stipularis*

One of the most attractive of the bush-peas, this shrub has massed flowerheads, 2–3 cm or more across, borne profusely at the end of branches. Individual flowers are yellow, enclosed in large, reddish-brown, papery bracts which add colour to the crowded flowerheads. The small, narrow, dark green leaves are numerous and have conspicuous stipules. A native of New South Wales, it grows to 2 m and is common in the Hawkesbury sandstone area.

9

Twining members of Fabaceae include *Hardenbergia* (3 species) usually purple-flowered and commonly known as Native Wistaria or False Sarsaparilla and *Kennedia* (about 13 to 16 species) the Coral Peas. Members of this genus are relatively large-flowered and include the vivid scarlet *K. prostrata* (Running Postman) and the black-and-yellow *K. nigricans* (Black Cockatoo flower). Another trailing pea plant is *Abrus*, of which Australia has only one species, *A. precatorius*, noted for its colourful seeds which are commonly called Jequerity Beans.

Gompholobium is a genus of about 25 species, confined to Australia and commonly known as Wedge Peas from the characteristic shape of the flowerbuds. Members are found in all States. Western Australia has 16, all endemic to that State; New South Wales has 8, some endemic, some extending to other eastern States. South Australia and Tasmania have one species each. The Wedge Peas are small erect shrubs. Leaves are alternate, and often in sets of three leaflets branching from a common base, like the fingers of a hand. Flowers are usually large; stamens are free and the keel sometimes has a fringe of fine hairs. With the exception of one purple-flowered and one blue-flowered West Australian species, they are all yellow to orange-red in colour — in New South Wales they are commonly called Golden Glory Peas. Pods are inflated, and round, or nearly so.

Plate 10.

JEQUERITY BEANS — *Abrus precatorius*

Pictured here are the bright scarlet, black-blotched, hard and shining seeds of the Jequerity Bean. Australian Aborigines used them as body ornaments and decorations for weapons. It is also probable that they used extracts from the seeds medicinally, particularly as a cure for trachoma (sandy blight). *A. precatorius* is found in the tropical north of Australia but is not confined to this continent, occurring also in other tropical areas of the world. It is a straggling climber on large trees. Small, pinkish-mauve flowers are borne in May. Seeds cling to the pods after they open. Leaves are fernlike, and close up at night.

Plate 11.

GOLDEN GLORY PEA — *Gompholobium* species

This is a handsome shrub, 1–2 m in height, a native of coastal sandstone areas of New South Wales and Queensland. Large, bright yellow pea-flowers, 2–3 cm or more across, are borne in late winter and spring.

Plate 12.

BLACK BEAN — *Castanospermum australe*

Flowers of this tall tree from rainforests of Queensland and the north coast of New South Wales are large, orange-red, and borne in loose clusters in early summer. Stamens are free, and protrude beyond the petals. Glossy, dark green, compound leaves are unequally pinnate, with individual leaflets usually more than 10 cm long. Woody, swollen pods, up to 20 cm long and 5 cm broad, contain chestnutlike seeds (the generic name is derived from *castanea*, chestnut, and *sperma*, seed, and the alternative common name is Moreton Bay Chestnut). These seeds have toxic properties and were used by Aborigines as fish poisons and medicines. They also used them as food, after first soaking them in water for several days. The tree is a source of a valuable and extremely beautiful cabinet wood.

10

11

12

FAMILY CUNONIACEAE

PERHAPS THE best-known Australian member of this family is the New South Wales Christmas Bush, *Ceratopetalum gummiferum*, pictured opposite.

The Cunoniaceae is a family of trees and shrubs almost entirely confined to the southern hemisphere. Flowers are usually small and white (in *Ceratopetalum* the calyx persists after the flower falls, enlarges, and becomes highly coloured). Leaves are usually opposite, and may be simple or compound, often trifoliolate. Stipules are always present and are often large and united in pairs.

Australia has about 35 representatives, mostly inhabitants of eastern rainforests. Many are important timber trees. The genus *Ceratopetalum* includes Coachwood (*C. apetalum*) which has colourful calyces rather like the Christmas bush, and is the source of a richly coloured, beautifully grained timber. Red Carabeen (*Geissois benthamii*), is a brush-forest tree of northern New South Wales and south-east Queensland; also known as Brush Mahogany and Red Bean, it is the source of a deep red cabinet wood. *Ackama* is a genus of three species, two endemic to Australia. These are the Roseleaf Marara and the Rose Alder, both of which produce a close-grained, rosy-brown timber (the third *Ackama* species is the New Zealand Maka-maka).

A well known member of the family is *Callicoma serratifolia*, the so-called Black Wattle. Leaves are large, dark green, serrated and woolly on the under-surface; flowers are tiny and crowded into fluffy globular heads resembling those of many *Acacia* species (wattles).

FAMILY THYMELAEACEAE

THIS IS a cosmopolitan family, most abundant in Africa and Australia but with representatives even in Arctic regions. It includes the sweetly scented daphne of old-world gardens, which was introduced into Britain from Japan in the 18th century. Many species have tough fibres, sometimes used in the manufacture of quality writing paper; Australian Aborigines used the bark from native species (notably the "banjine" of Western Australia) for making cords.

Four genera occur in Australia, the largest being *Pimelea*, with 80 endemic species. This genus includes the pincushion-like Riceflowers and the Qualup Bells of Western Australia.

Plate 13.

CHRISTMAS BUSH — *Ceratopetalum gummiferum*

In midsummer this shrub or small tree is ablaze with colour, but the bright blossoms are not flowers: they are ripening seed-pods. Tiny white true flowers appear in October; after they fall the calyx enlarges with maturity and changes in colour.

Plate 14.

SLENDER RICEFLOWER — *Pimelea linifolia*

This small eastern Australian shrub is in blossom almost all the year. Flowers are white, sometimes pink, and are borne in terminal heads, surrounded by 4 large bracts.

FAMILY COCHLOSPERMACEAE

Plate 15.

WILD COTTON — *Cochlospermum fraseri*

The large, bright-yellow flowers of this native of north-west Australia appear in spring. Fruit is a dry capsule, within which are seeds, clothed in soft, downy, cottonlike hairs. It belongs to the small but widespread tropical family Cochlospermaceae.

13

15

14

FAMILY PROTEACEAE

THE PROTEACEAE family is almost wholly confined to the southern hemisphere and has its greatest development in Australia. At one time it was believed, on the basis of fossil evidence, that Australian members of this family existed in Tertiary times in Europe and North America. This has since been largely discounted, but fossils of *Banksia* and other genera have been found in lignite deposits of the Oligocene epoch near Yallourn, Victoria.

The family is a large one, with over 60 genera and at least 1,500 species, of which 37 genera and more than half the total number of species are indigenous to Australia, some genera and practically all of the indigenous species being confined to this continent. South Africa, with about 600 species, is another major centre of development, and the family is also well represented in South America and New Caledonia. Only two species occur in New Zealand, and the only representatives in the northern hemisphere are a few species of the predominantly New Guinean genus *Helicia*, which range as far northward as India and Japan.

The family name is derived from Proteus, the mythical Greek sea-god who could change his form at will. It alludes to the amazing diversity found among members. Flowers, foliage, fruit, size, and habit differ greatly, even within the same genus. Banksias range from entirely prostrate shrubs with stems creeping underground and only the leaves and flowerheads appearing above the sandy soil, to trees up to 15 m in height. Leaves may be flat or cylindrical, entire or much-divided, short, broad,

continues on page 26

Plate 16.

WARATAH — *Telopea speciosissima*

The rich crimson flowerheads of this tall, many-stemmed shrub are 10–15 cm across. Each consists of numerous individual flowers, massed into a dense terminal head and surrounded by large, colourful bracts. Dozens of these spectacular blooms may be produced on a single bush, and in spring the rocky hillsides of its natural habitat blaze with vivid colour. Aborigines called it "waratah", a word which in their tongue meant "seen from afar". Robert Brown, the Scottish botanist who made the first extensive record of Australian plants while accompanying Flinders on *Investigator*, was intrigued by the aptness of the native name, and preserved it in the generic name, *Telopea* (from the Greek *tele*, afar, and *opos*, eye).

Telopea speciosissima is the New South Wales Waratah, confined to that State and occurring naturally on coastal hillsides and highlands around the populous cities of Sydney, Newcastle and Wollongong. Inevitably the magnificent natural stands which so captured the imagination of local natives and early botanist are becoming increasingly rare. Pictured opposite is a small corner of a stand covering more than 10 hectares at Duffy's Forest, near Sydney; when photographed it was already doomed to fall beneath the bulldozer's blade. On the other side of the coin, this is a plant which, once established, takes kindly to cultivation in suitable soil, and many magnificent specimens may be seen growing in Sydney gardens. It is the official floral emblem for the State of New South Wales.

The waratah is an erect shrub, varying in height from 1–4 m. Stiff, handsome, dark-green leaves, 10–15 cm long, have prominent veins and serrated edges. Fruit is an elongated woody capsule, and seeds are winged.

long, or narrow. In *Hakea* they vary from the small, needle-sharp, cylindrical leaves of the Dagger Bush (*Hakea teretifolia*) to those of *Hakea lorea*, the Cork Tree, which are up to 50 cm in length. *Grevillea robusta*, the Silky Oak, has large, fernlike, much-divided leaves; the western *Grevillea excelsior* has narrow, rounded, pinelike foliage.

Floral parts are in fours — the perianth petaloid, with 4 segments (tepals), usually tubular in bud, valvate, separating variously, becoming free, or leaving portion of the tube entire, or open on one side. The 4 stamens are situated opposite the flower-segments and attached to them, often completely fused so that only the anthers are free. The style is long and usually prominent above the flower. It may be straight or hooked, and in some cases the floral tube splits along one side allowing it to protrude in a characteristic loop while the stigma is still held. Within these bounds, however, lies the family's greatest diversity.

These simple, usually small flowers, may be arranged in spiralling spikes, up to 30 cm long, as in *Banksia*; in dense terminal heads, as in *Telopea*, the spectacular waratah; in slender racemes, as in *Grevillea*; or, more rarely, in umbels, as in the bizarre, symmetrical Firewheel, *Stenocarpus sinuatus*. Colours range from smoky-grey to iridescent green, from pale butter-yellow to glowing orange-gold, from dusty pink to vivid crimson.

Timber from members of the Proteaceae is remarkable for its unusual, silvery grain, and some of the larger trees, notably *Grevillea robusta*, the Silky Oak, are the source of valuable cabinetwood. *Macadamia bear edible fruit, commonly called* Popple nuts, cultivated commercially to some extent in Australia and on a much larger scale in Hawaii. Many species, particularly of *Banksia*, are valuable honey plants. Apart from these, the family is not of very great economic importance, and its main appeal is as a source of highly decorative and varied ornamental shrubs and trees.

continues on page 28

Plate 17.

DRYANDRA — *Dryandra polycephala*

The south-western corner of Australia is the oldest part of this continent and perhaps the most ancient land surface in the world. Plant life there, isolated by sea and desert, untouched by climatic or geological changes throughout countless aeons of time, has developed in a particularly individual way. Many species and some genera are entirely confined to the area, occurring nowhere else in the world. One such is *Dryandra*, a large genus of over 50 species, all restricted to the South West and some to a very limited section within that region.

Pictured is *D. polycephala*, a stiff, upright shrub 2–3 m high. Numerous bright-yellow flowerheads are borne in spring; leaves are most decorative, being long, narrow, and deeply toothed. It is confined to gravel areas of the Darling and Avon districts.

Dryandras have close links with the banksias. Flowers, usually various shades of yellow but in some species orange, red, pink, or even purple, are massed into round heads within a circle of bracts (in *Banksia* they are arranged in a spiral around a spike). Leaves are nearly always serrated, often grouped in a ring around the flowerheads. They vary greatly in length, width and pattern. In many species, such as the one pictured, they are long and narrow; in *Dryandra sessilis*, the Parrot Bush, they are short, broad and hollylike. Height and habit are also variable, ranging from prostrate shrubs to small trees.

17

Grevilleas, sometimes called Spider Flowers, form the largest genus in the family. They vary from prostrate trailing species to tall timber trees, up to 30 m high, but most are shrubby. With the exception of a few species in New Guinea, New Caledonia, and the Celebes, they are entirely confined to Australia. There are over 200 endemic species, and they are found in all parts of the continent, from the tropical rainforests of Queensland to the dry interior, from the islands of the Gulf of Carpentaria to Tasmania. By far the greatest number of species, however, occur in the south-west of Western Australia.

Flowers may be almost any colour except blue. They are arranged in loose racemes, short and radiating from the top of a common stalk in the typical "spider flowers", but sometimes in long spikes such as *Grevillea eriostachya* and *G. banksii* (pictured overleaf, plates 21 and 22) or one-sided, toothbrush-like sheafs, as in *G. pteridifolia* (plate 20, opposite) and *G. pungens* (plate 23, overleaf). Typical "spiderflowers" with umbel-like racemes *include G. speciosa* and *G. buxifolia* (plates 18 and 19, opposite) *G. oleoides* (plate 24, overleaf). Another example is *G. lavandulacea*, a low, sometimes spreading shrub from Victoria and South Australia which bears flowers ranging in colour from bright red to almost white, and has rigid, sharp-pointed leaves.

The style is long and slender, often hooked, and the floral tube usually splits down one side before the flower opens, allowing the style to protrude in a loop. This perianth tube may be straight, but is more often curved. As with other genera in the family, it is petaloid, and consists of 4 segments.

Leaves are alternate and may vary greatly in shape and size. Some are tough and leathery, some silken soft; some entire, others much-divided and fern-like in appearance; some are sharp-pointed, toothed or prickly.

Fruit is a small, often hairy, thin-shelled and brittle follicle, from which the style persists at the tip in a characteristic hook.

Plate 18.

RED SPIDER FLOWER — *Grevillea speciosa*

A circle of dainty, bright-red flowers, each with prominent, slender style much longer than the floral tube, make this one of the most decorative of the grevilleas. Usually a small shrub a metre or so high, it is very common in sandstone areas of the coast and tablelands of New South Wales. Flowers are borne throughout the year, but are most abundant in spring.

Plate 19.

GREY SPIDER FLOWER — *Grevillea buxifolia*

This striking grevillea has rusty-brown flowers, thickly overlaid with a fuzz of grey hairs and crowded into rounded, umbel-like racemes at the end of branches. Like *Grevillea speciosa*, it is a native of the coast and lower mountain areas of New South Wales, a small, bushy shrub, 1–2m high, bearing its quaint, attractive flowers for most of the year.

Plate 20.

GREVILLEA PTERIDIFOLIA

There is no common name for this grevillea, a native of monsoon country in the Northern Territory and tropical North Queensland. It is a small tree, up to 6 metres high, which in spring bears large, flame-coloured, one-sided flowerheads in spectacular profusion. Leaves are pinnate (featherlike) with individual leaflets very narrow and up to 10 cm long. The specimen pictured was photographed in November at Yirrkala, in remote Arnhem Land.

18

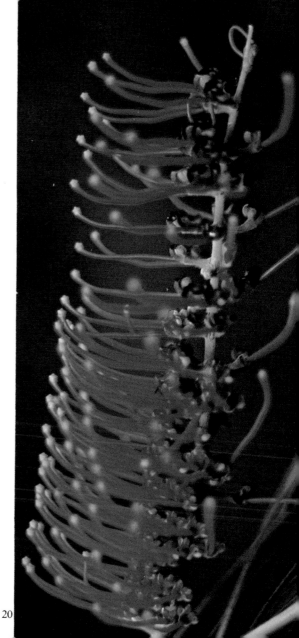

19

20

Plate 21.

GREVILLEA ERIOSTACHYA

The large, bright golden flowerspikes of this spectacular grevillea blaze like beacons on the red sand ridges and spinifex country of north-western Australia and the arid interior. It is a tall, rather straggly shrub which blooms profusely for many months, from early spring to late summer. Individual flowers are large and clothed in fine silken hairs. They are arranged in crowded, spikelike terminal racemes up to 15 cm long. Branches and flower stalks are covered with a hoary grey fuzz. Leaves are compound, consisting of 3 to 5 long, very narrow, sharp-pointed leaflets.

The specimen pictured was photographed in October, growing in typical sandplain scrub near Carnarvon, Western Australia. It is in this area that the shrub can be seen in greatest profusion, but its range extends southward to the region of Salt Lake Barlee and as far inland as Ayers Rock in the Northern Territory.

Plate 22.

BANKS GREVILLEA — *Grevillea banksii*

This grevillea is a native of Queensland, but it is well known and widely cultivated elsewhere. Bright, ruby-red flowers with prominent gold-tipped stamens are crowded into terminal racemes 10–15 cm long. Foliage is dense, and the large, grey-green leaves, silken-haired underneath, are fernlike and divided into long narrow leaflets. A bushy shrub rarely exceeding 3 m, it flowers profusely in spring and continues in bloom for many months. There is also a white-flowering form.

Plate 23.

GREVILLEA PUNGENS

This grevillea occurs in tropical north Australia, and was photographed flowering at Yirrkala, near Grove, Arnhem Land, in November. It is an erect shrub, 1–2 m high. Branches and foliage are covered with short, soft hairs. Rigid, stalkless, deeply lobed leaves, about 5 cm long, are much-veined on the upper surface and densely silken underneath. Flowers, rich glowing orange in colour, are borne in one-sided terminal racemes, 5–7 cm long.

Plate 24.

OLIVE GREVILLEA — *Grevillea oleoides*

The fiery red flowerheads of this small erect shrub are borne clustered profusely along all branches, either stalkless in the axils of leaves or on very short terminal branchlets. In this it differs from the closely related *Grevillea speciosa* (Plate 18) which bears its red spider-flowers in terminal heads at the ends of lateral branches. Leaves of *G. oleoides* are much longer than those of *G. speciosa*, and flowers are often larger.

The Olive Grevillea derives both botanical and vernacular name from the shape of the dark green leaves, which somewhat resemble that of the European olive leaf. It grows to about 2 m in height, and occurs in dry sclerophyll forest and along rocky and sandy river banks in the sandstone country south of Sydney. Flowering season extends from early spring to summer.

21

22

23

24

Banksias commemorate the name of Sir Joseph Banks, the botanist who accompanied Cook on his voyage of discovery and collected the first specimens of the genus in 1770 at Botany Bay. There are about 50 species, all confined to Australia except one, which extends to New Guinea. They are found in all States of the Commonwealth, occurring most abundantly in Western Australia, where there are 40 endemic species.

Slender, stalkless flowers are surrounded by velvety-brown bracts and borne in dense terminal spikes, containing as many as 1,000 individual blooms arranged in spiralling rows around a thick woody axis. Petals are silken-haired, very narrow, each with a spoonshaped lobe at the top, in which an anther is seated. The style is long and is released from the floral tube to form a characteristic loop while the stigma is still held captive.

These floral spikes develop into thick, woody fruiting cones, on which numerous withered flowers remain in a dry, bristly fuzz. Fruit is a large woody two-valved capsule containing two paper-thin, winged seeds. In the majority of species curiously few develop to maturity; those that do, protrude at scattered intervals, like heavy-lidded eyes among the bristles of the withered flowers — the quaint, hairy "banksia-men" of children's tales.

Banksias include some of the most fantastically decorative members of the Proteaceae. They range from prostrate shrubs with underground stems and flowers which appear to squat directly on the ground, to trees up to 15 m high with gnarled and furrowed butt a metre or more across. Flower-spikes, in some species 30 cm or more long, range in colour from glowing orange in *Banksia ericifolia* to vivid green in *B. robur*. The Western *B. coccinea* has scarlet, gold-tipped styles set in velvety-grey flowers; *B. violaceae*, a tiny 30 cm high shrub of the south-western sandplains, has purple flowerheads.

Leaves are tough and alternate. They range in size and shape from the large, leathery, prominently veined leaves of *B. robur*, 10–25 cm long and 5–8 cm broad, to the tiny heathlike foliage of *B. ericifolia*; from the glossy green "holly" leaves of *B. ilicifolia* to the deeply toothed, narrow and elongated leaves of *B. dryandriodes*.

All banksias produce nectar in abundance — they are commonly called "native honeysuckle" for this reason — and some are valuable honey plants. Aborigines made a honey drink by soaking the spikes in water; in country areas today children often collect the nectar by banging the copiously laden flowerheads against a dish. Honey-eating

continues on page 34

Plate 25.

SILVER BANKSIA — *Banksia marginata*

Also known as Tree Honeysuckle, this is a bushy shrub or small tree with narrow, blunt-tipped, dark green leaves, about 5 cm long, silvery underneath and tawny-tipped when young. It is common along the temperate east coast of Australia, extending to South Australia and Tasmania — the specimen pictured was photographed at Bruny Island, off the south-eastern tip of the island State.

Flowers are soft yellow, carried in short, oblong spikes rarely more than 8 cm long. They persist for some time as a brown, and finally grey, stiff hairy fuzz, but eventually fall, leaving the floral stalk clothed in soft, red-brown, velvety plush. This banksia blooms profusely from early spring to late summer, and is valued as a honey plant.

25

birds and bees abound when banksias are in bloom, the bees pushing their way in between the rows of flowers and running up the crowded spiralling avenues, collecting nectar as they go from storage places at the base of each flower.

Xylomelum is a genus of 4 species, all confined to Australia. These are the Woody Pears, remarkable for their large pear-shaped wooden fruit, up to 10 cm long and covered with soft velvety hairs, which splits along the upper side to reveal two flat winged seeds. Leaves are leathery, conspicuously veined, and may be entire or finely serrated along the margin. Flowers are carried in dense spikes in the leaf axils.

Perhaps the best known species is *X. pyriforme*, a small tree or large shrub native to Queensland and New South Wales and common in the Hawkesbury sandstone country. Numerous little yellow flowers are crowded in the axillary spikes. Young foliage is rosy pink, covered with velvety down. Bark is corky and deeply furrowed.

In startling contrast to the massive, woody and completely inedible "pears" of *Xylomelum* is the fruit of *Persoonia*, another genus of the family. This is a succulent, fleshy drupe, in many species edible — the "jibbongs" of the Aborigines, who gathered them for food; they are popularly called

continues on page 36

Plate 26.

HEATH-LEAFED BANKSIA — *Banksia ericifolia*

Throughout the cooler months of the year, from mid autumn to late spring, 30 cm long brushes, bronze to bright orange-gold, blaze like fiery torches amid the fine heathlike foliage of this eastern Australian banksia. It is a large bushy shrub or small tree, very shapely in habit, with tiny, stiff leaves, rich dark green in colour, 10–15 mm long, very narrow and densely crowded along the branches, the young foliage at the tips being noticeably lighter and brighter. Unlike those of most banksias, flowers usually open at the top of the spike first, particularly when the lower portion is shaded by thick foliage. The conspicuous bright orange styles are long and remain permanently hooked at the tip.

This banksia was one of the first Australian native plants sighted by Captain Cook and Sir Joseph Banks when they landed in Botany Bay in 1770. It was one of two *Banksia* specimens collected by Banks himself (the other was *B. serrata*). *B. ericifolia* is confined to New South Wales, and is very common in the Hawkesbury sandstone country around Sydney.

Plate 27.

SAW BANKSIA — *Banksia serrata*

These are the "old man" banksia trees of eastern Australia; they grow as high as 15 m, with stout, gnarled, knobbly trunk and dark, furrowed, pebbly bark. Flower-spikes, shorter and wider than those of *B. ericifolia*, are silvery green and velvety to touch in bud, later turning yellow when the flowers open fully, then orange-red as they wither. The hairy cobs are the traditional "banksia men", covered with a dense wiry fuzz of dead flowers from which protrude isolated large seed capsules, the size and shape of a pullet's egg and thickly clothed in soft, short, dove-grey to rusty red fur.

Stiff, dull-green, coarsely serrated leaves are 10–15 cm long and often hoary underneath. Young foliage on new growth is a soft and woolly, copper-pink, to rich reddish-brown in colour.

A native of Queensland, New South Wales, Victoria, and Tasmania, it is often seen growing in the most inhospitable situations, leaning out over bare stone on rocky hillsides. It flowers in summer, but the bizarre fruiting cones are retained for many years and these, combined with the attractive young foliage and decorative, twisted trunk and limbs, make *B. serrata* a tree of year-round interest.

26

27

Geebungs today. There are about 60 Australian and 1 New Zealand species, ranging from small trees to prostrate shrubs.

Flowers may be carried in terminal racemes, or solitary or in pairs in the leaf axils. They are small, regular, and cream or yellow in colour; the 4 perianth segments roll back, giving the flower a bell-like appearance and exposing 4 short stamens surrounding the straight style.

The Broadleafed Geebung, *P. levis*, is an eastern species, a tall shrub which grows up to 5 m high. Reputedly a very slow grower, its trunk and limbs are clothed in multiple layers of loose, papery bark, the outer layers rough, dark and often charred by bushfires, the inner ones bright pink and silky. Leaves are large, broad, and more or less distinctly 3-veined. Flowers are sometimes axillary, sometimes in racemes.

P. lanceolata, another eastern species, is the Lance-leaf Geebung, sometimes called Bonewood on account of the hardness of its timber. It grows to 2 m, and bark is hard and persistent. Flowers are always in the axil of a leaf. The Pine-leaf Geebung, *P. pinifolia*, a shrub 1–2 m high with weeping habit, has soft, fine foliage. Little bright-yellow flowers are carried in terminal racemes and fruits, the colour and size of grapes, are borne on the drooping tips of branches.

There are 5 endemic species of *Macadamia*, all confined to eastern Australia and occurring mainly in rainforests of Queensland and the north coast of New South Wales. Two species, *M. tetraphylla* and *M. integrifolia*, are cultivated commercially for their edible nuts, known variously as Popple nuts, Bobble nuts, and Queensland Bush nuts. *M. integrifolia* is confined to Queensland, but *M. tetraphylla* extends into New South Wales. A small bushy tree, it has long, dark green, glossy leaves, toothed at the margin and arranged in whorls. The little creamy-white to pinkish flowers are carried in long, slender, crowded sprays.

Plate 28.

SWAMP BANKSIA — *Banksia robur*

The brilliant, almost iridescent green flowers of the Swamp Banksia are carried in dense squat spikes, framed by a circle of young branches and stiff, deeply toothed leaves. The shrub is small, rarely over 2 m high, and bushy in habit. A dense coat of velvety red fur covers branches, leaf-stalks, and the prominent veins on the undersurface of the huge leaves, which when mature may be as much as 25 cm long and 8 cm wide. *B. robur* is a native of coastal New South Wales and, as the common name implies, grows in swampy situations. The specimen pictured was photographed in Kuring-gai Chase, near Sydney.

Plate 29.

ACORN BANKSIA — *Banksia prionotes*

This is a Western Australian banksia, confined to a limited area in the south-west within a radius of 300 km or so around Perth. A tree 6–9 m high, it grows in white sand and flowers in autumn and winter. Blunt-tipped flower-spikes are about 10–15 cm long; bright orange flowers contrast with woolly grey unopened buds at the top, giving the inflorescence an attractive, acorn-like appearance. Narrow, deeply serrated leaves are up to 30 cm long.

28

29

Hakeas are a group of over 130 species of shrubs and trees, all endemic to Australia and most confined to the west. Individual flowers are carried on short stems in axillary clusters or racemes along the branches. The slender floral tube splits along one side while still in bud, allowing the style to protrude in a loop; later the petal segments roll back and usually become free. Fruit is a large, very thick, hard, woody capsule, two-valved and often rounded, with a beaklike projection. Seeds are winged.

Leaves are alternate and, like those of other members of the Family Proteaceae, show considerable variation. In many species they are much reduced, cylindrical and sharp-pointed — hakeas are commonly called Needlebushes because of this — but in others they may be flat, entire, serrated, or divided.

Two closely related genera of the family Proteaceae are both commonly known as Drumsticks or Conebush. These are *Isopogon* and *Petrophile*. In both, numerous flowers are crowded in dense cylindrical formations around a woolly stem, each individual bloom being protected by a scalelike bract. These bracts overlap one another, and become enlarged as the flowers fade, so that the heads resemble a pinecone in appearance. In *Isopogon* this cone is round and woolly; the fruit, a small hairy nut, is embedded in the scales and falls off with them. In *Petrophile* the cone is elongated and the bracts remain persistent, in time opening out sufficiently to allow the small nutlets to shake loose.

There are over 30 species of *Isopogon*, and about 40 of *Petrophile*. Both genera are restricted to Australia, their greatest development being in the west.

Plate 30.

PINCUSHION HAKEA — *Hakea orthorrhyncha*

There are several western *Hakea* species with flowers clustered into rounded heads topped by long, conspicuous, yellow styles, the whole resembling a bright sea-urchin or colourful pincushion crowned with golden pins. Both names are commonly applied to them. The one pictured, *H. orthorrhyncha*, is a native of sand plains of the ancient land around Bonnie Rock, Western Australia. It grows to about a metre in height, and flowers in winter.

Plate 31.

DAGGER HAKEA — *Hakea teretifolia*

This is an eastern *Hakea*, with the typical cylindrical, sharp-pointed leaf which has earned so many of the genus the vernacular name of "needle-bushes". It is a straggling shrub, usually about 2 m high and common in eastern New South Wales, Victoria and Tasmania, often growing profusely in damp situations. The needle-like leaves are intimidating, but provide a haven for the small birds of the heathlands. It blooms in spring and summer, bearing creamy-white, nectar-filled flowers, clustered in spider-like groups in the leaf axils. The hard woody fruit has a strange, elongated shape, rather like a dagger or a kingfisher's beak.

Plate 32.

BOTTLEBRUSH HAKEA — *Hakea bucculenta*

Showy red bottlebrush flower-spikes, combined with long, fine, grasslike foliage, make this Western Australia hakea one of the most spectacular of the genus. It is a handsome shrub, growing to a height of about 3 m, and it flowers in August.

30

31

32

Plate 33.

DRUMSTICKS — *Isopogon anemonifolius*

I. anemonifolius, the species illustrated, is a tall erect shrub from the east coast of Australia, ranging from south Queensland to Victoria. The stiff leaves are much divided and cleft into recurring segments of three. Young foliage, flowers, bracts and fruit, are softly hairy. Flowers are bright yellow, and are borne for many months in spring and summer.

Plate 34.

HONEY FLOWER — *Lambertia formosa*

The long tubular flowers of *L. formosa* are filled with nectar, attracting the honey-eaters — birds, bees, and pigmy possums — and giving the plant its common name, Honey Flower. It is also called Mountain Devil because the fruit, a horned, sharp-beaked, woody capsule, gives a quaint impression of long ears and pointed snout.

Flowers are borne in groups of 7, surrounded by long, narrow, silky bracts, rosy pink to yellowish-green in colour. The floral tube is up to 5 cm long and the petal segments are tightly recurved at the tips, leaving the prominent styles protruding another 10–15 mm or so. Stiff, sharp-pointed leaves, shiny green on top and pale on the under-surface, are arranged in whorls of 3.

L. formosa is the sole eastern representative of the genus and is confined to sandstone areas of eastern New South Wales (the others, about 8 in all, are restricted to Western Australia). Its flowers may be seen at any time of the year, but are borne most profusely in spring.

Plate 35.

SMOKE BUSH — *Conospermum* species

The flowers of *Conospermum*, usually woolly, greyish-blue in colour and carried in dense spikes above the foliage, have inspired the vernacular name, Smoke Bush, but in some species flowers are pure white, bright blue, lilac, or pink. Leaves are always stiff, alternate and entire, varying in shape from long and broad to small, crowded and heath-like.

Flowers are stalkless, and contained within a broad, persistent, usually hairy bract. As with all Proteaceae the floral parts are in fours, but in *Conospermum* the 4 tiny lobes of the floral tube are unequal, the rear one being much larger than the others. Fruit is a small hairy conical nut, tufted at the top.

Plate 36.

FIREWHEEL TREE — *Stenocarpus sinuatus*

These fiery wheels, up to 10 cm or more in diameter, are borne in glorious profusion in late summer and autumn. Each consists of about a dozen waxy red flowers radiating from the tip of a common stalk. This spokelike formation is maintained while the stigma is held captive within the floral tube; when finally released, the styles spring upward in a tangled mass of glowing colour.

The Firewheel tree grows as high as 30 m in its natural habitat, the rich coastal brush forests of Queensland and northern New South Wales.

Under cultivation it is considerably smaller. Leaves are large, glossy green, wavy at the margins, and often deeply lobed.

35

34

36

FAMILY PITTOSPORACEAE

THIS LARGELY Australian family includes a host of attractive climbing plants, twining under-shrubs and shapely trees, many with sweetly scented flowers. There are 9 genera, all of which occur in Australia. All are endemic except *Pittosporum*, which has a wide distribution in warmer areas of Africa, Asia, New Zealand and the islands of the Pacific. Flowers, of various colours, have 5 petals, 5 sepals, and 5 stamens. Leaves are simple, alternate, and usually glossy. Fruit is a capsule or a berry.

Pittosporum, the largest genus and the only one to extend beyond Australia, has about 160 species. Nine occur in Australia, and all except one of these are confined to this continent. Australian *Pittosporum* species are trees or large shrubs; they are to be found in all States and the Northern Territory. Flowers are small, often bell-shaped, and are borne in clusters. Most are highly perfumed. Fruit is an orange, berrylike capsule, within which seeds are embedded in a sticky, resinous substance (the generic name is derived from the Greek *pitta*, resin, and *spora*, seed).

A closely related genus, *Hymenosporum*, has only one species, *H. flavium*, the sweetly scented Native Frangipani of eastern Australian rainforests. Flowers are larger than in *Pittosporum*. Fruit is a brown, flattened capsule. Seeds are winged and not sticky. The Aborigines called it Wollum Wollum and it is also known as Coin Pod because of the characteristic winged seeds in flat, thick cases.

Marianthus, a genus of about 15 prostrate or twining undershrubs, is confined in the main to Western Australia, though eastern States have some representatives. The attractive flowers, popularly called Marybells, are blue, white, or various shades of red. Fruit is a capsule and seeds are dry. *Billardiera* differs from *Marianthus* mainly in the fruit, which in *Billardiera* is a fleshy, edible berry, slightly acid in flavour and known colloquially as Appleberry, Blueberry, and Dumplings.

Plate 37.

MOCK ORANGE — *Pittosporum undulatum*

Heavily scented, small white flowers, dark green, glossy leaves, and bright orange fruit, have given this small tree its popular name. The perfume is strongest at night, and the flowers are moth-pollinated. A native of eastern States, it flowers in late winter and is now extensively cultivated.

Plate 38.

ORANGE MARYBELL — *Marianthus ringens*

This decorative climber from Western Australia bears clusters of pendulous, orange-red, bell-shaped flowers in spring. Large, leathery leaves are a deep, glossy green.

FAMILY POLYGALACEAE

Plate 39.

MATCH HEADS — *Comesperma ericinum*

The lilac flowers of this slender, dainty shrub are borne on loose terminal panicles in winter and spring. They bear a superficial resemblance to pea-flowers (family Fabaceae) but the "butterfly wings" are not petals at all, but large, colourful sepals. The common name refers to the shape of the buds. *Comesperma* is an entirely Australian genus of herbs, climbers, and small shrubs, belonging to the worldwide family Polygalaceae. There are about 24 species, many endemic to the west, though the one pictured occurs in eastern States.

37

38

39

FAMILY STERCULIACEAE

THE KURRAJONGS

THIS IS a widely dispersed family, occurring mainly in tropical regions and particularly abundant in Australia and South Africa, though fossil evidence indicates that in ancient times its range extended far beyond the present boundaries, into colder regions such as Alaska. It is a family of shrubs, herbs, and trees, and is closely related to the Malvaceae (Hibiscus family). There are some 50 genera (about half of them indigenous to Australia) and over 1,200 species.

Cocoa and chocolate are extracted from the seeds of a central American species, *Theobroma cacoa*. Cola is obtained from *Cola acuminata*, a native of west Africa. Some species yield valuable gums, others (notably those of the genus *Heritiera*) are the source of useful cabinet timber. Many are cultivated for their ornamental appeal.

Flowers may be either bisexual or unisexual and sometimes all types — male, female, and bisexual flowers — are borne on the same plant. Floral parts are in fives. There are 5 sepals, usually large, petal-like, and fused into a colourful 5-lobed, bell-shaped calyx, 5 petals, always very small and sometimes absent altogether, and 5 to 15 stamens. The ovary is often 5-celled and the style 5-branched.

Leaves are alternate, sometimes covered with fine, starlike, branching hairs. They are simple, (rarely compound) entire, or deeply lobed, frequently into 5 divisions. Stipules are often present, and if so are usually deciduous. Fruit is a woody capsule.

Perhaps the best known Australian genera are *Brachychiton, Lasiopetalum*, and *Thomasia*, all of which are entirely confined to this continent.

Brachychiton, a genus of about 12 species, includes the spectacular Illawarra Flame Tree, *B. acerifolium*, (pictured). *B. discolor*, the Lacebark (so-called because the thick bark of the fully-grown tree has an unusual, lacelike texture) bears large panicles of bright pink bell-flowers backed with soft red-brown fur. Both these are tall rainforest trees of eastern Australia. The Kurrajong (*B. populneum*) is widespread, growing from southern Victoria to Queensland and flourishing on the dry inland plains. It bears creamy-white, pink-throated bell-flowers, velvety soft on the outside and chocolate-spotted within.

continues on page 46

Plate 40.

FLAME TREE — *Brachychiton acerifolium*

The brilliant red flowers of the Flame Tree are borne over a long period, from early spring to late summer. When in full bloom, the dark-green, shiny leaves are dropped, and the whole tree blazes as though aflame. A native of eastern Australian rainforests, from the Illawarra district of New South Wales northwards into Queensland, it grows as high as 30 m in its natural habitat.

The bell-shaped flowers have no true petals, but consist of 5 petal-like, bright coral-red, fused sepals. They are borne in panicles, each branching stalk being as brightly coloured as the flowers themselves.

Leaves are variable. In the young tree they are often palmate (deeply divided into 5 lobes, like the fingers of an outstretched hand) but in older trees they are usually entire, and more or less oval in shape. The thick bark of fully grown trees is furrowed in a lacy pattern. Fruit is a large, woody, boat-shaped capsule.

The fantastic Bottle Tree (*B. rupestre*) is confined to inland (but not arid) areas of Queensland. It grows to 20 metres in height and stores water in a huge, bottle-shaped trunk, sometimes 2 m in diameter.

There are over 20 *Lasiopetalum* species. They are commonly called Velvet Bushes because of the soft velvety hairs, often rusty-red in colour, which in many species cover branches, foliage and flowers. All are shrubs. *L. ferrigineum*, a native of New South Wales, is known as "Rusty Petals", and *L. rufum* as "Red Velvet".

Thomasia species are the so-called Paper Flowers; petals are absent or minute and the dilated, colourful sepals are dry and papery-thin. There are about 30 species, all confined to the west except one, which extends to South Australia and Victoria.

Other Australian genera of interest are *Commersonia* and *Heritiera*. *Commersonia* has about ten species and include the strong-fibred "Blackfellow's Hemp" (*Commersonia fraseri*). This species is found in damp situations on the margins of rainforests and along the banks of creeks and rivers, its range extending from eastern Victoria to southern Queensland. A tall shrub or small tree, it is the source of long, tough fibres which the Aborigines used to make cords for fishing and hunting nets. Leaves, up to 15 cm long, are heart-shaped, sometimes ovate-lanceolate, and often sharp-pointed, with margins irregularly toothed or, rarely, lobed. Flowers are creamy white, and carried in loose, cymose panicles.

Heritiera is a genus ranging from south-east Asia to Australia, where it is found in the rainforests of the eastern coast. The species are large trees, much buttressed at the bole, and are the source of timber valued for cabinet work and veneers. One such is the Red Tulip Oak of north-eastern Queensland. Some species have at times been placed in the genera *Tarrietia* or *Argyrodendron*.

Plate 41.

BRACHYCHITON species

The *Brachychiton* species pictured here is a far cry from the giant Flame Tree of eastern rainforests (*B. acerifolium*, plate 40). Photographed at Nourlangie Rock, in Arnhem Land, Northern Territory, it is a low woody shrub which appears dead but for the colourful flowers on its bare branches. No leaves can be seen because the shrub is deciduous; flowers are borne before the new growth appears each season.

Australian Aborigines found *Brachychiton* species a valuable adjunct to their way of life. They used the sweet and succulent young roots of some species for food, obtained water from the swollen trunks of the Bottle Tree (*B. rupestre*), and used the tough fibres from the bark of many species to make fishing nets and dillybags.

Plate 42.

LARGE PAPER FLOWER — *Thomasia macrocarpa*

This tall erect shrub is a native of Western Australia, and occurs on the Darling Range near Perth, its range extending southwards down to Cape Naturaliste. Leaves are large, broad, heart-shaped and very hairy. Flowers are borne in spring and summer; the colourful papery "petals" are actually large tissue-thin, dilated sepals.

41

42

FAMILY MALVACEAE

GARDEN FAVOURITES such as hollyhock, *Hibiscus* and *Abutilon*, the Chinese Lantern-bush, belong to this family. So do the cotton plants of commerce (*Gossypium* spp.). The Malvaceae is a large family of herbs, shrubs, and soft-wooded trees, widespread over most of the world and particularly abundant in tropical America. It is closely related to the Bombacaceae (to which family belong the fantastic Baobab tree of northern Australia and the kapok of commerce) and there has been some botanical "swopping" of genera.

In colder regions the Malvaceae occur mainly as herbs, but in warmer areas there are some quite large trees. *Lagunaria patersonia*, the Pyramid Tree or Norfolk Island Hibiscus, a native of Queensland and Norfolk Island, grows as high as 12 m. It bears pink hibiscus-like flowers and is valued for its white timber.

The petals of Malvaceae flowers are contorted in bud and usually close up at night. Often large and colourful, they are typically darker in hue at the centre. There are 5 petals and 5 sepals; in many species the style branches into a 5-lobed stigma. Stamens are numerous, and united at the base into a close-fitting column around the style. Leaves are alternate, entire, or divided, often palmately (into 5). Fruit is a capsule or schizocarp, often 5 valved.

The largest genus is *Hibiscus*, with about 200 species, 30 or so of them indigenous to Australia. They are widespread across the continent (none occurs in Tasmania) and include some very ornamental flowering plants.

Gossypium, the cotton genus, is also well represented (some Australian species have at times been classified into separate genera). The well-known Sturt's Desert Rose (*G. sturtianium*) is widespread in the arid interior and has been adopted as the floral emblem for the Northern Territory.

Plate 43.

LILAC HIBISCUS — *Hibiscus huegelii*

Australia has many lovely native *Hibiscus* species, mostly in the warmer tropical areas, though this one is a native of South Australia and central and southern areas of the West. A shapely shrub which grows to about 2–3 m it bears large lilac-blue flowers from late winter to summer. Petals, 8–10 cm long, are slightly twisted in a spiral fashion, rather like the propellors of a boat; the dark-blotched base, common in flowers of this family, is mostly absent. Bright green leaves are roughly hairy, scalloped at the margins and deeply lobed, usually into five divisions.

Plate 44.

DESERT ROSE — *Gossypium* species

Australian members of the cotton genus, *Gossypium*, are plants of the hot, dry country, and are commonly called Desert Roses for this reason. They are widely distributed across the continent from the east coast of Queensland to the central and north coast of Western Australia. All bear hibiscus-like flowers, and most Australian species have pink to mauve petals with dark crimson to purple centres, a colour not found in members of the genus outside this country.

48

44

43

FAMILY EPACRIDACEAE

THE AUSTRALIAN HEATHS

THE EPACRIDACEAE is a family of heathlike shrubs and a few small trees, mainly confined to Australia and closely allied to the true heath family of the Old World (Ericaceae). There are 28 genera and about 350 species.

The family name, from the genus *Epacris*, means "on a hill-top" (Greek *epi*, on; *akris*, hill-top) and refers to the fact that these plants are often found on stony ridges. They show special adaptation to dry conditions (though some species are found in swamps). Leaves are mostly stiff, small and crowded, often sharp-pointed or thickened at the tip. An unusual feature is the apparently parallel venation, similar to that of a blade of grass — actually veins are not parallel in the true sense but diverge from the same point at the base of the leaf.

Flowers are regular, and floral parts are in fives. Petals are always united into a tube, with 5 free lobes. This floral tube is usually long, sometimes swollen in the middle so that the flower is cuplike rather than bell-shaped or tubular. Occasionally it is so short as to be little more than a ring, as in *Epacris microphylla* (Plate 47). The lobes at the tip of the corolla may be short (*E. longiflora*, Plate 45), or they may be spreading, giving the flower a starlike appearance. In *Styphelia* (Plate 46) they are rolled back tightly. The 5 stamens are in most cases attached to the petals. Fruit is usually 5-celled, and is either a capsule or a berrylike, succulent drupe — Aborigines gathered many of the latter type for food.

The largest Australian genus is *Leucopogon*, with about 150 endemic species. These are the "White-Beards", so-called because the inside surface of petal-lobes is densely clothed with white hairs. Other genera are *Sprengelia*, the Swamp Heaths (3 species), *Styphelia* ("Five Corners") with about 15 species, *Richea*, a genus of 9 species largely confined to alpine regions of Tasmania, and *Epacris*, which consists of about 30 species and is confined to eastern Australia and New Zealand. *Epacris impressa*, the Pink Heath, is the official floral emblem for the State of Victoria.

Australian heath-flowers are usually white or some shade of pink, or red, but yellow, green, and rarely blue flowers are also seen. The main flowering season is long, from midwinter to midsummer, and some species seem to be in bloom almost continuously throughout the year.

continues on page 52

Plate 45.

FUCHSIA HEATH — *Epacris longiflora*

The scarlet and white pendulous flowers of this lovely native of eastern Australian sandstone country are borne almost continuously throughout most of the year. They are 2–3 cm or more long, and are carried in the axils of stiff, sharp-pointed, triangular little leaves, often in a one-sided fashion along the full length of the slender branches. It is a straggly little shrub, usually growing to about a metre but occasionally higher.

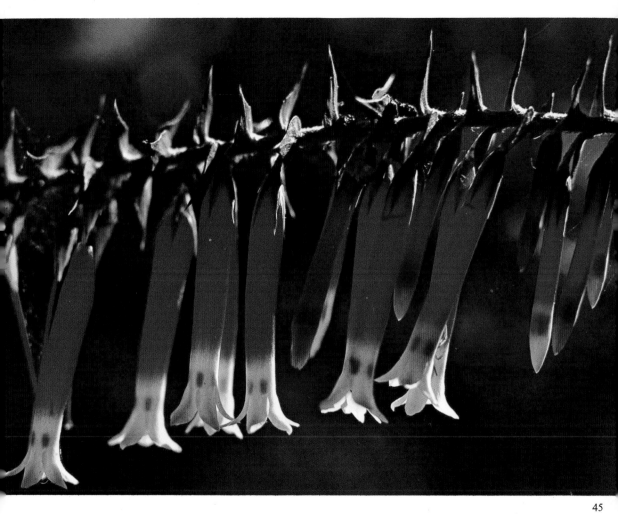

Styphelia is a genus of about 15 prickly-leafed shrubs in the family Epacridaceae. They occur in all States and are characterised by prominent, protruding stamens and tightly rolled-back petals of tubular flowers. The petal-lobes are bearded on the inside, though not so densely as those of *Leucopogon* ("White-Beards"). Leaves are rigid, sharp-pointed, stalkless or nearly so, and flowers are borne in the leaf-axils. Fruit is a succulent drupe with a 5-cornered stone. It is edible, and Aborigines gathered it for food.

The sandstone country of coastal New South Wales is a major centre of development, and 6 *Styphelia* species occur there. The one pictured is *S. tubiflora*, the Red Five-corners.

Other interesting New South Wales species are *S. viridis* and *S. longifolia*, both of which bear green flowers (the former species extends to southern Queensland). Most widespread in distribution is *S. adscendens*, the Golden Five-corners, which occurs in drier areas of New South Wales, Victoria, Tasmania, and South Australia. The 4 Western Australian species are endemic and all occur in the southern portion of that State. Most colourful is *Styphelia hainesii*, which bears long scarlet flowers in winter. It is confined to a limited area around Esperance, on the southern coast.

Plate 46.

RED FIVE-CORNERS — *Styphelia tubiflora*

The Red Five-Corners is an erect, bushy shrub which carries dainty, ruby-red, slender flowers in winter and spring. First described by botanist Sir James Smith (*A Specimen of the Botany of New Holland,* 1793), it was cultivated in England as early as 1802.

Plate 47.

CORAL HEATH — *Epacris microphylla*

Coral heath grows in sandy and swampy areas of eastern New South Wales and Queensland. The small flowers, usually snowy white but occasionally tinged with pink, are crowded profusely along stiff branches throughout winter and early spring. The 5 petals are fused into the typical tubular corolla of the Australian heaths, but in this species the floral tube is little more than a ring — very short and relatively broad. The petal lobes are longer than the tube and widespread, so that the tiny flowers have a starlike appearance.

E. microphylla is a small shrub, often only 15 cm or so high and rarely more than a metre. The little, sharp-pointed, heart-shaped leaves are crowded, and flowers are borne in the leaf-axils.

FAMILY MYRTACEAE

THE MYRTACEAE is the largest family of flowering plants in the flora of Australia. It includes the traditional gumtrees (*Eucalyptus* spp.) so dominant in the Australian landscape — only in the rainforests and the near-desert areas of arid interior are they absent or overshadowed by a greater abundance of other genera. The bottlebrush-flowers of *Callistemon* and *Melaleuca* belong to the Myrtaceae; so do the teatrees (*Leptospermum* spp.) so-called because Captain Cook's sailors made a "concoction" from the leaves of one species; also the button-headed kunzeas, the giant lillypillies of the rainforests, and many, many others. In all there are more than 50 Australian genera and well over 1,000 species, all woody but ranging in size from small prostrate shrubs to huge trees. *Eucalyptus regnans*, the Mountain Ash, is the world's tallest flowering tree, rivalled only by the giant redwoods of California.

The family is represented in warmer parts of both hemispheres, but there is a remarkable development of types peculiar to Australia and indeed it has been suggested that the Myrtaceae may have originated here and migrated elsewhere before the land links with the rest of the world were severed. Although there is little definite evidence to support this, it is a fascinating thought. If it is true some of these emigrant myrtles now return from abroad in the form of cloves, dried flowerbuds of an East Indian *Eugenia* — the "spices of the Orient" — which have played a major part in human intercourse since earliest times.

A striking feature of many members of the Myrtaceae is the role of the stamens in the attractiveness of the flowers, even when petals are present and fairly large. Stamens are mostly long and numerous; petals are frequently small and sometimes absent. In some groups of *Eucalyptus*, the petals are fused in bud to form the operculum or cap (the generic name, from the Greek *eu*, well; *kalyptos*, covered, means well-covered). In other groups the operculum consists of fused sepals, or there may be an outer cap of sepals and an inner one of petals. This cap is forced off when the flower opens; it is shed altogether and the crowded, often colourful stamens are the most conspicuous feature of the gum blossom. In the bottlebrush flowers of *Callistemon*, once again the stamens play the prominent part. Petals are tiny, pale-coloured, or greenish, often deciduous and always inconspicuous — the flowerheads are showy because of the numerous long stamens.

The family can be divided into two distinct sections: the Myrtoideae, with berrylike fruit such as the Australian eugenias, *Acmena* and *Syzygium* species — the lillypillies and brush cherries; and the Leptospermoideae, the fruit of which is a dry, often woody capsule — the familiar gumnut is a typical example.

The Myrtoideae are mainly tropical in distribution. South America is the major centre of development (the allspice of commerce is the dried, unripe berry of a Central American species), and most Australian genera of this sub-family are to be

continues on page 56

Plate 48.

SCARLET-FLOWERED GUM — *Eucalyptus ficifolia*

This spectacular flowering gum, one of the most widely cultivated and best known of the eucalypts, occurs naturally only in a very limited area of a few square miles in the extreme south-west corner of Western Australia. It is a small to medium-sized tree with rough, scaly, reddish-brown bark. Flowers are borne in late summer in large terminal clusters, carried outside the foliage and often completely covering the crown of the tree with brilliant scarlet.

48

found in the warm, moist rainforests of the east coast.

The vast majority of Australian members however, belong to the sub-family Leptospermoideae, which is almost exclusively Australian — there are only minor extensions eastwards to New Zealand and New Caledonia, and northwards to Indonesia, the Philippines, and Malaysia. Members are typically the heat-resisting plants of dry places, and are characterised by many adaptations to conserve moisture. Fruit is a dry capsule. Leaves are tough, with thick cuticles, often hairy, reduced or crowded. Many hang vertically, turned sideways to the sun's rays. Oil glands are usually present.

The largest Australian genus is *Eucalyptus*, with at least 400 species. It embraces trees ranging in height from 1–100 m, from desert mallees to *E. regnans*, the mighty Mountain Ash, tallest hardwood in the world.

Eucalypts predominate in more than nine-tenths of Australia's total forest area. They range over vast extremes of climate and country, from hot tropical areas to sub-alpine regions, from rich coastal plains to parts of the dry interior. The genus is almost exclusively Australian. Only half a dozen species occur naturally outside this country, and these are confined to New Guinea and nearby islands to the north. None occurs in New Zealand.

Economically the group is of great importance. It includes many of the world's best hardwoods, and some eucalypt timbers are used extensively in the manufacture of pulp, paper, and hardboard. Many are important honey trees, valued as a source of both nectar and pollen. Leaves of some species yield valuable essential oils, and the kino (gum) has some pharmaceutical use as an astringent. Scores of very lovely eucalypts are extensively cultivated both in Australia and abroad. In addition to their ornamental appeal they are prized as hardy wind-breaks and soil-binders — some drought-resistant, some tolerating waterlogged swamps, others withstanding

continues on page 60

Plate 49.

PINK-FLOWERED IRONBARK — *Eucalyptus sideroxylon*

Also known as Mugga Ironbark, this is a slender upright tree with deeply furrowed, almost black, bark and dull green leaves. It can grow to 15–20 m, but is more often smaller. Flowers vary from bright pink to white. They are carried in groups of 7 (or 3 in the sub-species, *tricarpa*) springing from a common stalk. It is a native of eastern Australia and flowers in spring.

Plate 50.

LINDSAY GUM — *Eucalyptus erythronema*

Shown here are the buds of *E. erythronema*, an attractive small eucalypt which grows naturally in heavy clay soil in the Swan River district of Western Australia. Bark is smooth and light grey in colour; leaves are rather long and pale green. It flowers in late summer, bearing masses of deep red flowers which are characteristically carried in groups of three on bright, almost blood-red stalks. This photograph shows the distinguishing feature of *Eucalyptus* species: the operculum or cap of fused petals and sepals which rests on the rim of the calyx tube and protects the flower in bud. Later it is thrust off by the crowded radiating rows of stamens which constitute the familiar "gum blossom".

Plate 51.

BUSH ROSE — *Eucalyptus rhodantha*

The Bush Rose is a small mallee very closely related to the Mottlecah, *E. macrocarpa*, and is possibly derived from hybridisation between that species and another. Like the Mottlecah, it has very large crimson flowers carried singly in the axils of decorative, silvery-grey, stem-clasping leaves. This species is one that retains juvenile-type foliage in maturity; leaves are opposite, arranged more or less in fours along mealy branches. Pictured is the fruit ("gumnut"), in this species up to 8 cm across. It is formed by the ripening calyx tube and bears the scar of the fallen operculum around the rim.

50

49

51

Plate 52.

CUP GUM — *Eucalyptus cosmophylla*

The Cup Gum occurs naturally in a limited area of South Australia, from the Mount Lofty Ranges to Encounter Bay and Kangaroo Island offshore. It varies in size from a dwarf shrub to a rather straggling, smooth-barked tree, 10 or more metres high. Creamy-yellow flowers are borne on short stalks in clusters of 3, from autumn to early winter. The calyx-tube is cup-shaped, hence the common name, and the petal-cap of the pale yellow, red-flecked buds is peaked. Leaves are broadly lance-shaped, thick, and stiff. This is a tree which often grows in swampy places, and on Kangaroo Island, where the specimen pictured was photographed, it is commonly called "Bog Gum" for this reason.

Plate 53.

FOUR-WINGED MALLEE — *Eucalyptus tetraptera*

The bright-red, four-cornered calyx tube of the Four-winged Mallee is almost 8 cm long, and the red petal-caps are also angular, so that the buds are almost diamond-shaped. It is a low, straggling shrub from that remarkable area for Australian flora, the south-west of Western Australia. Thick, shining, bright green leaves are red-stalked and often up to 30 cm long; they are carried on strikingly angular branches.

The Fuchsia Mallee, *Eucalyptus forrestiana*, has large, orange-red, angular buds, rather similar to those of the Four-winged Mallee, but the crowded stamens, when released, are bright gold.

It is found in the same area of south-west Western Australia, but its range extends further inland than that of the Four-winged Mallee. It grows naturally in dense thickets, individual trees being slender and only a metre or so high, and flowers in late summer, often continuing in bloom into autumn and early winter.

Plate 54.

PINK-FLOWERED BLUE GUM — *Eucalyptus leucoxylon*

This is a winter-flowering eucalypt, native of South Australia and parts of western Victoria and New South Wales, and commonly found on heavy alluvial soil or clay. It was photographed flowering in the Barossa Valley, South Australia, in July. Though occasionally small and mallee-like in growth, it is normally quite a large tree. The trunk is usually smooth, mottled white and blue, with a varying amount of dark, rough bark at the butt. Flowers are borne on long stalks, usually in groups of 3. An alternate common name is Yellow Gum.

Several other eucalypts are also called Blue Gums, perhaps the best known being the Tasmanian Blue Gum, *Eucalyptus globulus*, regarded as the official floral emblem of that State. It is an extremely fast-growing tree which can attain a height of over 60 m (this fast growth has been used as a means of reclaiming swampy land, a well-known example being its use in the draining of the Pontine Marshes, near Rome, in the 1930s). Mature leaves are spectacular, 30 cm or more long. Blossom is creamy-white.

Plate 55.

STRICKLAND'S GUM — *Eucalyptus stricklandii*

This eucalypt is sometimes called the Yellow-flowered Blackbutt, because of its bright yellow flowers and the dark, rough bark at the base of the otherwise smooth pale trunk. It grows in the goldfields area of Western Australia, east and south of Kalgoorlie, on poor laterite soils and hilly situations, rarely exceeding 10 m in height, and flowers from November to January.

52

53

54

55

prolonged exposure to snow and extreme cold.

Eucalypts are commonly grouped according to bark, timber, or other convenient features. Many species, chiefly those with smooth bark, are called Gums — rather a misnomer since no true gum is obtained from any eucalypt. The sticky, dark red exudation seen in many is kino, a resinous material containing tannin. It is particularly abundant in some rough-barked eucalypts which are commonly known as Bloodwoods for that reason.

Peppermints are a group of eucalypts with strongly aromatic foliage, in some cases the source of commercially valuable essential oils. Ashes have pale timber, lighter in weight than most eucalypts and somewhat like that of the European ashes. Wood of the Boxes is hard and durable, resembling that of the European box. Ironbarks have dark-coloured, rough, deeply furrowed and corrugated bark on the trunk and large branches. Stringybarks have bark of a lighter colour, close, fibrous, and very durable, which hangs in long loose strings and will pull away from the trunk in strips.

Mallee is the term applied to many scrubby eucalypts tending to develop numerous slender stems rather than one main shaft. These spring from a much-enlarged woody rootstock (ligno-tuber) and the mallee form of growth is the tree's answer to harsh conditions of soil or rainfall, bushfires, and extremes of heat and cold. Many mallees are noted for the size and brilliance of their flowers.

In most *Eucalyptus* species leaves of young saplings are vastly different to those of the mature tree. Juvenile leaves, often bluish-grey in colour, quite often broad and stalkless, are always more or less opposite. In certain species, such as *E. rhodantha* (Plate 51) this juvenile foliage is retained throughout the life of the tree, but in the majority of species it is progressively discarded and replaced with mature leaves which are typically sickle-shaped, stalked, and mostly alternate. They are tough, usually hang vertically, and have a pronounced marginal vein. If the tree is damaged by bushfire or cutting, the sucker regrowth reverts to the juvenile foliage, and both types are frequently seen on the same tree.

A closely related genus is *Angophora*, with seven species, all found in eastern States, where they are commonly known as gumtrees or apple-gums. The main characteristic which distinguishes *Angophora* from *Eucalyptus* species is the presence of separate petals and sepals, rather than the eucalypt's characteristic cap-like operculum. Also, *Angophora* leaves are always opposite and "gumnuts" are always ribbed, whereas most eucalypts have alternate leaves and ribbed fruit is the exception rather than the rule.

Callistemon is a genus of about 20 species of shrubs and small trees in the family Myrtaceae. They are to be found in all States, but New South

continues on page 62

Plate 56.

TROPICAL WOOLLYBUTT — *Eucalyptus miniata*

Photographed here blooming near Nourlangie Rock, Northern Territory, is the colourful, winter-flowering Tropical Woollybutt. These brilliant orange flowers are usually in groups of 7 and radiate from a central point like the spokes of a wheel. Each individual flower is about 2 cm long, and the gumnuts which follow are elongated and ribbed in a rather square-sided fashion. This is one of the most common eucalypts in the Northern Territory, and its range extends westwards to the Kimberleys and eastwards into northern Queensland. Usually a tree grows to 10 or 12 m, it is occasionally taller and sometimes much smaller and shrublike. Bark is scaly and persistent at the butt, and the small broad leaves are leathery.

56

Wales, with 16 species, is the main centre of development. Numerous individual flowers are carried in dense, cylindrical, "bottlebrush" spikes at the tips of branches. The shoot continues growing from the apex, and downy new foliage soon protrudes beyond the flower-spike — a characteristic also of many bottlebrush-flowered Melaleucas. The following season a new flower-spike forms at the growing tip, and the woody cuplike fruit of the earlier flowers remains clustered in solid masses lower down the branch. These capsules remain on the tree indefinitely — in many cases they do not open and release seed unless the branch or plant is damaged — and the age of the specimen can usually be counted by the successive clusters.

Flowers of *Callistemon* are often vivid crimson or scarlet, but may also be white, creamy-yellow, pink, mauve, or even pale green. There are 5 very inconspicuous petals. The numerous free stamens are colourful and much longer than the petals, and the attraction of the inflorescence lies in them: the generic name is from the Greek *kallos*, beauty, and *stemon*, stamen. Leaves are usually long, narrow and stiff, alternate and often crowded.

The closely related genus *Melaleuca* has more than 150 species, all Australian and all confined to this continent except one, which extends to the East Indies. This is *M. leucadendron*, the Cajeput Tree, from which comes the cajeput oil of commerce. The genus reaches its greatest development in Western Australia, where there are about 100 species, most of them endemic.

As with *Callistemon*, there are 5 small petals, but in *Melaleuca* the prominent, colourful stamens are not free, but are united at the base into 5 bundles, which are placed opposite the 5 petals. Flowers may be arranged in bottlebrush spikes, like those of *Callistemon*, or in rounded heads or small clusters along the stems and at the ends of branches. Colours range from white, through yellow, orange, and various shades of pink and mauve, to brilliant crimson. Leaves are variable — sometimes opposite and sometimes alternate, ranging from tiny and crowded to large and broad.

A characteristic of most species of *Melaleuca* is the spongy, papery bark, which can be stripped off in layers — they are commonly called Paperbarks for this reason. The generic name, from the Greek *mel*, black, and *leuca*, white, aptly describes them because the outer bark of the trunk is often black, charred by bushfires, while inner layers and bark on branches are usually white.

Kunzeas belong to the myrtle family. There are about 25 species, all confined to Australia and about half of them endemic to the west. Flowers

continues on page 64

Plate 57.

CRIMSON BOTTLEBRUSH — *Callistemon citrinus*

This is a red bottlebrush, plentiful on the east coast of Australia from Queensland to Victoria, a colourful shrub often found in swampy places and common around Sydney. Flowerspikes are up to 12 cm long and the rigid, narrow, pointed leaves are lemon-scented and vary in length from less than 2 cm to over 5 cm. It is a straggling shrub, 1–2 m high; flowers are borne for long periods, from late winter to summer.

Plate 58.

SWAMP PAPERBARK — *Melaleuca deanei*

The flower-spikes of *M. deanei* are about 5 cm long and are borne in summer. It is a small shrub, rarely more than a metre or so high, found on wet heathlands of the Hawkesbury sandstone country around Sydney. There are several eastern melaleucas commonly called swamp paperbarks; one, *M. quinquenervia*, actually grows in the brackish water of coastal swamps, attaining a height of up to 20 metres.

57

58

have 5 petals, but these are always small and the numerous stamens are always considerably longer; stamens are free, as in *Callistemon*. Kunzeas are mostly heathlike shrubs, rarely small trees. The main flowering season is spring and summer, and colour of blossoms may be white, pink, mauve, red, or yellow. Leaves are mostly small, narrow, and alternate. Fruit is a capsule, dry or succulent, but not woody. Usually 3-celled, it opens at the top and is crowned by the persistent sepals.

Darwinia is a genus of over 30 species, mostly confined to Western Australia but with some representatives in South Australia and eastern mainland states. None occurs in Tasmania. It differs from most other members of the Myrtaceae in that stamens are not the main floral attraction, but are small and inconspicuous. In *Darwinia*, bracts around the flowers and often the pistils are showy. The style, often bearded, extends well beyond the floral tube, and flowers are often clustered into close heads at the ends of branches, giving the inflorescence a pincushion appearance. In a very limited area, the Stirling Ranges of south Western Australia, there are several *Darwinia* species in which the flowerheads are surrounded by enormous, colourful bracts, forming bell-flowers up to 5 cm long. These are the Mountain Bells, and each main peak in the range has its own distinctive species.

Plate 59.

BREAD AND JAM FLOWERS — *Darwinia fascicularis*

Flowers of *Darwinia fascicularis* are white when they open, later turning pink and then deep red as they mature. They are tubular, with 5 tiny petals, 5 even smaller sepals, and 10 short, relatively inconspicuous stamens. The decorative "pins" are the elongated styles of pistils, a rather unusual feature in members of this family (Myrtaceae). Individual flowers are arranged in clusters of about 6 or more, and these clusters are usually in groups. Flowers do not mature in a mass, but successively, giving the bush its quaint, two-toned effect and incidentally ensuring that the honey-sucking birds which visit them can transfer fresh pollen from younger flowers to the mature stigmas of older ones in the same cluster. It is a native of eastern New South Wales.

Plate 60.

PINK BUTTONS — *Kunzea capitata*

The little rounded buttonlike flowerheads of this *Kunzea* are carried at the end of short, twiggy branches. They consist mainly of crowded, rosy-pink to mauve, gold-tipped stamens; the individual flowers have 5 petals, but they are much smaller than the stamens. It grows in sandstone country of eastern Australia, rarely exceeding a metre in height.

Plate 61.

PINK FEATHER FLOWER — *Verticordia picta*

This is a little shrub, less than 60 cm high, which grows on the sand-plains of south-western Australia and bears its bright pink, fringed flowers in spring. There are about 50 *Verticordia* species, all except a handful confined to Western Australia. They are typical of the sand-plains and are commonly called Feather-flowers because of the characteristic fringe of long hairs on the calyx.

Plate 62.

SILKY KUNZEA — *Kunzea pulchella*

Bright ruby-red flowers and silken, silvery-grey leaves make this *Kunzea* (formerly known as *K. sericea*) one of the most attractive of the genus. A native of southern Western Australia, it grows on granite, often finding a foothold in crevices in bare rock. Its range extends from around Lake Moore in the north to Esperance on the south coast and the nearby Recherche Archipelago offshore.

59

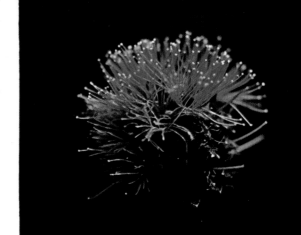

60

61

62

Plate 63.

SMALL-LEAFED FRINGE MYRTLE — *Calytrix microphylla*

These starry flowers are borne for long periods from early autumn to late spring. At first pink, they turn mauve, then white, as they mature. *Calytrix microphylla* is a small tree, growing to about 5 m in stony ground of north-western Australia, from the Kimberleys to Arnhem Land. The specimen picture was photographed at Port Essington, Northern Territory.

There are about 40 *Calytrix* species, mostly small shrubs and all confined to Australia, the majority of them to the west, though one or two species occur in every State. Flowers have 5 star-like petals, alternating with 5 sepals; the latter are joined together at the base to form a shallow cup and taper off at each lobe into a long, fine, hairlike point. Stamens are numerous. Fruit is a small nut surmounted by the persistent calyx, which remains after the petals drop, enlarging and changing colour often in quite spectacular fashion as the fruit matures.

Plate 64.

WOOLLY TEA-TREE — *Leptospermum lanigerum* var. *macrocarpum*

Flowers of *Leptospermum* species have 5 petals, alternating with 5 sepals, and numerous stamens arranged in a single whorl and always shorter than the petals. The ovary is usually 5-celled, and the style arises from a depression at the summit. There are about 40 species, and they are represented in all States, though New South Wales is the main centre of development. The genus is not confined to Australia, but occurs also in New Zealand (where many colourful hybrids have been developed from the indigenous red-flowered species) and in the islands north of Australia. Most are shrubs; some are small trees. Flowers may be white, pink, or red; leaves are alternate, aromatic and usually small.

The Woolly Tea Tree, *L. lanigerum*, is so-called because the calyx of the flower is covered with long hairs. Foliage and branches are also woolly. The variety pictured (var. *macrocarpum*) is common in the Blue Mountains west of Sydney. It is a low, spreading shrub, rarely more than a metre high, but flowers are spectacular and larger than usual in this genus. They are remarkable for the conspicuous bright green ovary, a centimetre or more across. The fruit that follows is also large, being 2–3 cm in diameter.

FAMILY LECYTHRIDACEAE

Plate 65.

Careya species

This tree occurs in tropical northern Australia and was photographed flowering in November at Arnhem Bay. The large showy flowers are borne a few together in very short cymes. There are four petals and numerous stamens, which may be up to 5 cm long, though often much smaller. Leaves are up to 10 cm.

FAMILY LORANTHACEAE

THE MISTLETOES

THE MISTLETOE family is most abundant in tropical regions but is found in temperate zones as well. Members are semi-parasitic, attaching themselves to branches or, rarely, roots of other plants, and drawing water and mineral nutrients from the host. All have green leaves however, and manufacture their own food by photosynthesis.

There are about a dozen Australian genera, embracing over 60 species. These include two endemic, monotypic genera which grow as trees or shrubs attached to the roots of the host, rather than as many-branched shrubs attached to the limbs of trees. One is the most spectacular of the family: *Nuytsia floribunda*, the Western Australian Christmas Tree (plate 66); the other is *Atkinsonia ligustrina*, a bushy shrub up to 2 m high which is found only in a limited area of the Blue Mountains, near Sydney, New South Wales.

The conventional epiphytic mistletoes seen hanging in pendulous fashion from branches in the Australian bush are all indigenous. In many cases each species is found chiefly on a particular genus of host-tree — eucalyptus, acacia, casuarina — and sometimes seems to mimic the foliage of its host. Flowers are often brightly coloured and are a source of nectar for honey-sucking birds; the little red-breasted mistletoe bird feeds on the ripe berries.

The genus *Amyema* has about 30 Australian species. They occur in eastern States and the majority are endemic. Long-stalked flowers, usually yellow and red, are borne in pendulous or erect clusters of 3. *A. cambagei* has cylindrical, needle-like leaves; its favoured host is *Casuarina*. The Drooping Mistletoe, *A. pendula*, has long, narrow, lanceolate leaves; its hosts are chiefly *Eucalyptus* species. Other *Amyema* species are restricted to certain acacias, and seem to simulate the shape and colour of their hosts' foliage. Another genus found in eastern Australia is *Notothixos*. One species is a small shrub, unusual in that its host is nearly always another mistletoe! This is *N. subaureus*, which ranges from eastern Victoria to Queensland. Foliage is densely coated with golden hairs. Leaves are oblong to lanceolate. Flowers are minute, and carried in clusters from a common stalk.

Plate 66.

WESTERN AUSTRALIAN CHRISTMAS TREE — *Nuytsia floribunda*

In December *N. floribunda* blazes with glorious colour. Orange-gold flowers, carried in racemes up to 30 cm long, almost completely obscure the foliage. Though a member of the Mistletoe family, and semi-parasitic, it grows as a stout-trunked tree, anything up to 12m high and often in apparent isolation. It secures water and certain nutrients by tapping the roots of neighbouring plants, and while *Banksia* appears to be its favoured host, it has also been known to grow in association with much smaller plants, such as grass. *N. floribunda* is a native of the south-western province of Western Australia, where it is also known as the Swan River Blaze Tree. Leaves are thick and narrow, up to 8 cm long. Branches are brittle, and wood is soft and spongy.

FAMILY RUTACEAE

THE BORONIAS

THIS FAMILY includes the rue of medieval times — symbol of repentance and Shakespeare's "herb of grace", the curry-plant of Ceylon, and the citrus fruits — lemon, lime, cumquat, tangerine, orange, and grapefruit. However more than half of its members belong to warm temperate parts of the southern hemisphere, and of these the majority are indigenous to Australia — many of them endemic. They are also abundant in South Africa, where most of the remaining southern species are to be found. In the main these southern members of the Rutaceae belong to the tribe Boronieae, though Australia does have its own native citrus (*Microcitrus* spp.).

All members of the Rutaceae, from tangerine to boronia, from rue to curry to the tall rainforest trees such as Australian Teak, have one easily recognisable factor in common — highly aromatic foliage and the presence of oil glands which can be seen as tiny translucent dots when the leaves are held up to the light. Another clue to identity is the superior lobed ovary (seedbox) which is elevated on a disc rather like a tiny crown on a cushion.

Flowers of Rutaceae mostly have 4 or 5 sepals (calyx segments) and an equal number of petals. This is often a guide to identification of species. *Boronia*, for example, has 4 sepals and 4 petals; *Eriostemon* has 5. Leaves may be alternate or opposite — in *Boronia* they are opposite, in *Eriostemon*, alternate. Flowers are of many colours, often pink but also white, yellow, red, brown and, rarely green, or blue. They are frequently sweetly scented. Sepals are often united at the base to form a cuplike calyx. The 4 or 5 petals are mostly spreading in a starlike fashion, but in *Correa* they are united into a tube and in some

Boronia species are arranged in a bell-like manner. Stamens are either equal in number to the petals, or double in number; they are rarely more numerous. In the genus *Diplolaeana* many small flowers with bright stamens are crowded into heads surrounded by petal-like bracts, so that the whole resembles a many-stamened single flower.

Largest Australian genera are *Boronia*, with 60 to 70 species, *Eriostemon* and *Phebalium* with about 40 each, and *Zieria*, which has over 20. *Flindersia* (the generic name commemorates Matthew Flinders) is a genus of some 14 species found mainly in eastern Australian rainforests. It includes some valuable timber trees, notably Queensland Maple (*F. brayleyana*) and Australian Teak (*F. australis*). *Geijera*, a small, chiefly Australian genus of 5 species, includes useful fodder plants of dry areas — the Wilga (*G. parviflora*) and Sheepbush (*G. linearifolia*).

Plate 67.

WESTERN ROSE — *Diplolaena dampieri*

There are only 6 *Diplolaena* species and all are confined to Western Australia. Numerous brightly coloured yellow, orange, or red flowers are crowded into pendant heads and enclosed by a double row of greenish, petal-like bracts. *D. dampieri* (pictured) was one of the few Australian native plants collected by Dampier in 1699, and is described in his account of the voyage. It grows on sand dunes and is pictured here flowering in October at Cape Naturaliste, in the south-west.

Plate 68.

NATIVE MAY — *Phebalium squamulosum*

This Phebalium is a native of coastal eastern Australia, from Queensland to Victoria. Tiny, bright-yellow flowers are borne in crowded clusters at the ends of branches; long, prominent stamens are gold-tipped. Leaves are narrow, 2–7 cm long, shining dark green above and silvery on the under-surface. It is a spring-flowering shrub, ranging in height from 0.5–2 m, sometimes erect and sometimes spreading in habit.

With the exception of one New Zealand species, endemic to the North Island, Phebaliums are confined to Australia. New South Wales, with 8 endemic species, is the main centre. They are shrubs or small trees, with foliage often hairy or covered in little rough scales. Leaves are alternate.

Plate 69.

PINK WAX-FLOWER — *Eriostemon australasius* (formerly *lanceolatus*)

One of the largest-flowered of the Eriostemons, this has waxy pink petals up to 10–15 mm long. Individual flowers, 2–3 cm across, are borne profusely along branches in winter and early spring. Leaves, up to 8 cm long, are greyish-green and narrow. It occurs along the east coast of Australia, from Victoria to Queensland, and is particularly prolific in the Hawkesbury sandstone country around Sydney.

In *Eriostemon*, leaves are always alternate, simple and entire. Oil glands are prominent. Flowers, usually some shade of pink, sometimes almost white, have 5 waxy petals, 10 stamens, and a 5 lobed calyx. They are mostly widespread and starlike, borne solitary in leaf axils or at the ends of branches. *Eriostemon* differ from the closely related *Crowea* (a genus of 4 species) only in the absence of hairs on the anthers.

Plate 70.

NATIVE FUCHSIA — *Correa reflexa*

The Native Fuchsia is a very variable shrub; it grows from 0.5–1.5 m high, usually in sandy heathlands and forests, often near water. The rough, stem-clasping leaves are heart-shaped to oval, and flowers vary from red, with yellow tips, through greenish-yellow, and white, to entirely green. It occurs in South Australia, Victoria, Tasmania, New South Wales and Queensland, and flowers in late spring and summer.

The genus *Correa* is exclusively Australian; there are 11 species, occurring in all States except the Northern Territory. South Australia, with 7 species, has the greatest diversity. Leaves are simple and opposite. Foliage is leathery, and often hairy. Flowers, which may be white, yellow, green, pink, or red, have 4 calyx lobes (united into a small cup), and 4 elongated velvety petals, usually fused into a tubular bell with 4 lobes; there are 8 stamens.

Plate 71.

MAUVE PHILOTHECA — *Philotheca salsolifolia*

Philotheca is a small genus of 5 species, 3 of them confined to the west. They are closely related to *Eriostemon* and *Phebalium*, the main difference being that in *Philotheca*, stamens are not free but are united into a tube at the base. They are mostly heathlike undershrubs with small, crowded leaves. Flowers are 5-petalled, pink, mauve, heliotrope, or red.

P. salsolifolia, the species pictured, is a native of Queensland and New South Wales. Starry, pinkish-mauve flowers are borne singly at the ends of branches; foliage is fine and very crowded. It grows to about a metre and flowers in spring and summer.

68

70

69

71

Boronia is the largest genus in the family Rutaceae; none occur outside this continent, and about half of the species are confined to the west. Leaves are opposite, simple or divided. Foliage is highly aromatic. As with the eucalypts, the pungent odour of crushed *Boronia* foliage is the epitome of the Australian bush. Strong, at times even rank, it is the almost inevitable accompaniment of many a bush walk, stimulating and rousing the senses, calculated to bring nostalgic tears to the eyes of any exiled Australian.

Many bear highly-perfumed flowers. *Boronia serrulata*, the sweet-scented Native Rose of Hawkesbury sandstone country around Sydney, can often be detected some distance away by its perfume. It is now uncommon in the bush, having suffered from the fact that its limited range includes a large and populous city. Native Rose has rose-pink, cup-shaped flowers and diamond-shaped, stem-clasping foliage. The Western Australian Brown Boronia (*B. megastigma*) has a delightful and very powerful perfume. It occurs in a limited area in the south-west, and in its natural state grows in very wet soil. Flowers are cup-shaped, rich chocolate-brown outside and lemon-gold within. This is perhaps the best known of the boronias, and is widely cultivated in Victoria, so much so that it is often called "Melbourne Boronia".

Boronias are all shrubs, though one, *B. muelleri*, (commonly called Tree Boronia), has been known to grow more than 6 m in the rich damp soil of mountain forests in Tasmania and Victoria. Most *Boronia* flowers are pink, but some are white, and quite a few western species are blue, brown, or yellow. Floral parts are in fours — 4 sepals, 4 petals, 8 stamens. The deeply lobed ovary has 4 segments. The calyx is small, and forms a plate-like support for the flowers. Petals are free, often widespread in starry fashion but sometimes incurved at the tips in a cupshape.

The genus *Boronia* has close affinities with *Zieria* and *Eriostemon*, but species can be easily distinguished: *Boronia* species have 4 petals and 8 stamens; *Zieria* only 4 stamens, and *Eriostemon* 5 petals and 10 stamens.

Plate 72.

SOFT BORONIA — *Boronia mollis*

The Soft Boronia, a tall shapely shrub up to 2 m high, is a native of coastal New South Wales. It grows in cool shady situations, frequently on creek banks or the borders of rainforests. The soft leaves are pinnate (featherlike) and the undersurface and stem are covered with fine hairs. They have a strongly pungent aroma when bruised. Flowers are deep pink, and the short stamens are bright yellow.

Plate 73.

PINNATE BORONIA — *Boronia pinnata*

In late winter and spring this boronia bears large clusters of pale pink, waxy, semi-cupped flowers at the ends of slender branches. It occurs in all States except Western Australia, growing to about 2 m or even 3 m in cool moist gullies, but is considerably smaller and more compact in habit on poorer sandstone ridges. Some forms grow very close to the sea and will tolerate salt spray; indeed, under natural conditions the species may be found in any type of country from open heathland to deep shady gullies. The glossy-green, finely divided foliage is not as strongly aromatic as that of most boronias.

73

72

FAMILY RUBIACEAE

This large and almost cosmopolitan family has its main development in tropical areas. It includes *Coffea arabica*, from which comes the coffee beans of commerce, *Cinchona* spp., the "fever barks" from which quinine is derived, and the highly perfumed ornamental shrub, *Gardenia*.

Members include trees, shrubs, climbers and herbs. The family is characterised by opposite leaves, simple and usually entire, with stipules which are usually on the stem between pairs of leaf-bases and are sometimes leaflike, so that it appears the plant is carrying leaves in whorls. Flowers are regular, mostly with 4 or 5 corolla-lobes and the same number of alternate stamens. Ovary is inferior, with a single style. Fruit is a capsule, berry or drupe.

Two interesting genera with Australian representatives are *Myrmecodia* and *Hydnophytum*, tropical epiphytes which develop grotesquely swollen stems, in the spongy flesh of which ants take up residence, using the labyrinth of channels and chambers within the porous tuber as a readymade nest — they are popularly known as "ant-house plants" for this reason. Several species of *Myrmecodia* occur in tropical north Queensland; two, *M. muelleri* and *M. beccarii*, are apparently endemic. There is 1 indigenous species of *Hydnophytum*.

Coprosma is a genus of shrubs in the Rubiaceae. Its main centre of development is New Zealand — *C. repens*, the Looking-glass or Mirror plant, is a wellknown example. This fast-growing shrub owes its common name to its shining, glossy-green leaves; it thrives in sand and is often planted as a hedge near the sea front, flourishing in the face of salt spray. *Coprosma* species have unisexual flowers, usually occurring on different plants.

Flowers are insignificant, though the male flowers often have long drooping stamens. The fruits, however, are bright and berry-like drupes, in some species edible. Australian representatives include the Rough Coprosma, *C. hirtella*, and the Prickly Currant bush, *C. quadrifida*, found in moist fern gullies and mountainous areas of eastern Australia from Tasmania to New South Wales. Both have conspicuous, fleshy, orange-red fruit. Two species found on the high plateaux of alpine areas are the blue-berried *C. moorei* and the scarlet-berried Shining Coprosma, *C. nitida*.

Plate 74.

LEICHHARDT TREE — *Nauclea orientalis*

The strange and beautiful flower of the Leichhardt Tree, pictured here, was photographed blooming beside the Mitchell River, Cape York Peninsula, in November. *N. orientalis* is a handsome tree, with broad leaves 10 cm or more long. Bright yellow flowers are borne in dense rounded heads 2–3 cm in diameter, topped by long and prominent styles. Fruit is united into a hard, globular mass, pitted, rough, and more than 2–3 cm in diameter. Aborigines used an infusion of the bitter bark to stupefy fish and medicinally to induce vomiting as a cure for stomach disorders and snakebite. Bushmen use it as a substitute for quinine in the treatment of fevers. *N. orientalis* belongs to the family Rubiaceae.

FAMILY RANUNCULACEAE

THE BUTTERCUPS

THIS FAMILY derives its name from the Latin *ranunculus* — "little frog" — an allusion to the preference most members have for damp places. It has a wide distribution in cool and temperate regions of the world, being particularly abundant in the northern hemisphere, and includes many lovely garden flowers — larkspur, delphinium, columbine, love-in-a-mist, anemone, and peony.

Members are climbers or herbs, the herbaceous types having leaves alternate or in a rosette at the base, while the climbers have opposite leaves. Flowers usually have 5 sepals (sometimes more or less) and 5 petals, though petals may be absent and sepals petaloid, as in *Clematis*. They may be unisexual or bisexual; stamens are usually numerous, carpels often also, with styles frequently persistent in a hook or plume. There are 5 indigenous Australian genera; *Ranunculus*, with over 30 species, is the largest.

Plate 75.

TRAVELLERS' JOY — *Clematis aristata*

Clematis species often grow near water, thereby earning the vernacular name, "Travellers' Joy". They are woody climbers which ramble over shrubs, fallen logs and creek banks, clinging by means of modified leaf-stalks. *C. aristata* has long-stemmed opposite leaves consisting of 3 broad, toothed, lancelike or heart-shaped leaflets, each of which may be up to 8 cm in length. Large, creamy-white, starry flowers, 2–3 cm across, are borne in tangled clusters. They are unisexual, and usually the male and female flowers are borne on separate plants. There are no petals; the showy flowers consist of 4 long, narrow, petal-like sepals enclosing numerous silky stamens or slender, plumed styles, depending on the sex of the individual flower — occasionally bisexual flowers occur and sometimes all three types are borne on the one plant. When the flowers mature, the styles persist as long, curved, feathery appendages on the tightly clustered little dry fruit — rather like a hoary beard, inspiring the alternative common name, "Old Man's Beard".

Clematis has a worldwide distribution, but the 5 Australian species are all endemic. *C. aristata* is mainly a coastal and tableland species. It occurs in all States and is shown here clambering over fallen brush and a cycad in the Pemberton area of south-west Australia.

Plate 76.

MOUNTAIN BUTTERCUP — *Ranunculus graniticola*

Buttercups are water-loving plants, found mostly in marshy ground or near water. Many of them are high country perennials, blooming amid melting snowdrifts in spring and early summer. Leaves are usually lobed or much-divided; they may be alternate, but frequently spring in a tuft from the base of the plant, surrounding the long-stemmed, solitary flowers. Typically there are 5 brilliant, shining gold petals, but colour and number may vary: the largest Australian species, *R. anemoneus*, has numerous fragile petals of dazzling, almost transparent, white. The species pictured here, *R. graniticola*, is an alpine buttercup, photographed in early summer on the slopes of Mount Northcote, near Mount Kosciusko, New South Wales.

Plate 77.

KOSCIUSKO BUTTERCUP — *Ranunculus dissectifolius*

This buttercup is one of the rarer alpine species, occurring only on the slopes of Mount Kosciusko and the adjoining peaks of the Australian Alps. Stems and the much-divided leaves are clothed with long, fine hairs. Petals range from 5 to 10 or more.

75

76

77

FAMILY NYMPHAEACEAE

THE WATERLILIES

Waterlilies belong to the family Nymphaeaceae. They are aquatic plants, widely distributed in tropical regions of the world. Starchy rootstocks are submerged in the mud of shallow freshwater pools, and flat, round, hollow-stemmed leaves float on the surface. Flowers are usually carried slightly above water; they have 4 sepals, numerous radiating petals, and crowded stamens. Fruit is fleshy. Australia has 4 native *Nymphaea* species, and the Indian Lotus-lily, *Nelumbo nucifera* (now usually placed in a separate family, Nelumbonaceae), extends to our tropical north.

The best known and most widespread of Australian waterlilies is *Nymphaea gigantea*, pictured here flowering near Tully, north Queensland. Its range extends from the north coast of New South Wales through Queensland and the Northern Territory to the north-west of Western Australia. Flowers, usually blue but occasionally pure white, pink, or mauve, are borne in profusion on the seasonal lagoons of the tropical north; seeds remain dormant in the dry periods and are capable of withstanding prolonged drought. Nomadic Aborigines seek these seeds and the starchy tubers for food; they use the hollow leaf-stalks as breathing tubes when hunting game. Flowers may be up to 30 cm in diameter, and the round to heart-shaped leaves much larger.

Plate 78.

GIANT WATERLILY — *Nymphaea gigantea*

FAMILY PORTULACACEAE

This is a family of herbaceous plants, usually succulent and sometimes becoming woody at the base. Members are found in temperate and tropical parts of the world, the main centre of development being America.

Flowers are usually brightly coloured, and some species, notably those of *Portulaca*, are cultivated as garden ornamentals. Australia has several indigenous species of *Portulaca*, most of them endemic. Included is the almost cosmopolitan *P. oleracea*, prolific in the islands of the Pacific and valued as a food source by the indigenous inhabitants. Australia's nomadic Aborigines also prize it; the small seeds are washed and ground, and the succulent leaves are eaten raw.

The majority of Australian species, however, belong to the genus *Calandrinia*, a predominantly South American group with its main development in the desert areas of Chile. Australia has 30-odd indigenous species, nearly all endemic.

Plate 79.

PARAKEELYA — *Calandrinia* species

When the seasonal rains fall in the arid inland of Australia, the bare red sand and stony wastes bloom in unbelievable profusion of brilliant colour. Among the most prolific and spectacular of these desert plants are *Calandrinia* species, fleshy herbs belonging to the family Portulacaceae (the Aborigines called them "Parakeeyla" and used their succulent leaves for food).

Flowers are often large and showy, carried on slender stems arising from the centre of a rosette of leaves. Fragile petals, usually 5 in number, vary in colour from purple to white. Stamens are bright gold, and the style is branched. Fruit is a small capsule.

FAMILY AIZOACEAE

Plate 80.

NOON-FLOWERS — *Disphyma australe*

This little native succulent grows in saline soil of sea-marshes and inland salt-pans. It clambers over sand dunes and wave-splashed rocks along the coastline of temperate Australia from Queensland to the West, and carpets great areas of the interior around the dry salt lakes. Stems are prostrate and root from the nodes, enabling the plant to subdue shifting sand. Fleshy leaves store water, and because of this the plant can withstand prolonged dry periods. Flowers vary in colour from pink to purple; they are borne on slender stems, up to 8 cm long, springing from a basal cluster of rounded leaves.

D. australe is pictured here growing on the sandy margin of salt Lake Carmody, near Hyden, Western Australia. A member of the Pigface family (Aizoaceae) it is exclusively Australian and the only species in the genus, differing from the closely allied genus, *Carpobrotus*, mainly in that the flowers are stalked and the mature fruit is a dry capsule (fruit of *Carpobrotus* is a succulent, edible berry).

An interesting and rather curious fact about *Disphyma* and other members of this family is that there are no true petals. The shining colourful ring of soft fine filaments consists of flattened, petal-like stamens. These surround the inner circle of fertile stamens, opening widely in bright sunlight (hence the botanical name and its vernacular equivalent, "Noon-flower") and closing at night or in dull weather.

FAMILY AMARANTHACEAE

THE PLANTS of this family are small shrubs or herbs, occasionally climbers, with simple, entire leaves. Flowers are usually stalkless within dry, papery bracts; in most genera they are carried in dense, congested heads. The family is widespread in tropical and sub-tropical regions of the world, particularly Africa, America, and Australia. It includes garden favourites such as love-lies-bleeding (*Amaranthus caudatus*), cockscomb (*Celosia*) and bachelor's buttons (*Gomphrena*).

Several genera are represented in Australia (including *Amaranthus* and *Gomphrena*) but the great majority of indigenous species belong to the wholly Australian genus, *Ptilotus*. There are over 100 *Ptilotus* species (including those formerly classified as *Trichonium* — the two genera have now been united). They are herbs or small shrubs of the hot dry regions, with alternate, often hairy leaves. Papery flowers, sometimes brightly coloured, are covered in soft, feathery hairs and borne in densely packed terminal heads or spikes. Aborigines called them "mullamulla", early settlers "lamb's tails" or "featherhead"; all three names are still in common use.

Plate 81.

MULLAMULLA — *Ptilotus macrocephalus*

The rounded fluffy flowerheads of this mullamulla are up to 8 cm in diameter. They are shining white, tinged with green and tipped with gold. Leaves are long and narrow. The plant, a perennial, rarely exceeds 50–60 cm in height. It occurs in Western Australia, South Australia, the Northern Territory, and western parts of New South Wales and Victoria.

Plate 82.

FEATHERHEAD — *Ptilotus exaltatus*

The purple-flecked flowerheads of this species may be up to 15 cm long and 5 cm across. Leaves are greyish-green, rather thick and rigid, and 8–12 cm in length. An erect, stiff perennial, it grows up to a metre high, and occurs in all mainland States and the Northern Territory. (Photographed here near Derby, in the Kimberleys area of Western Australia).

80

81

82

FAMILY GENTIANACEAE

THE GENTIANS

The family Gentianaceae includes some of the most beautiful plants of highland meadows and alpine slopes. There are comparatively few southern members (New Zealand has the greatest number of species) and the family is most abundant in mountainous regions of the northern hemisphere, where grows the traditional gentian, famous for the intense blue of its flowers; the Australian gentian is closely related, and was once included in the same genus (*Gentiana*).

However, southern gentians are now classified in a separate genus, *Gentianella*. They differ from the northern group in various ways: anthers are versatile and veins on the petals are more numerous; petals do not have small lobes between them, as in *Gentiana*. Australia has only one *Gentianella* species, *G. diemensis* (pictured); it is abundant on alpine slopes, sometimes descending to sea-level.

Other genera found in Australia are *Centaurium* and *Villarsia*. *C. pulchellum*, the Australian Centaury, is a swamp-dwelling plant; it bears showy, rosy-pink flowers for long periods, from spring to late summer; vegetative parts contain a bitter principle which has been used medicinally. *Villarsia* species are marsh-flowers, water plants which grow near creeks, on lagoons, swamps and shallow billabongs. They have bright golden flowers and waterlily-like leaves. There are 8 Australian species, all confined to Western Australia and most of them endemic to that region.

Other Australian genera include *Limnanthemum* and *Sebaea*. The family consists mainly of erect, tufted, annual or perennial shrubs, and waterlily-like aquatics. Leaves are generally in opposite pairs, and the inflorescence is usually cyamose, though sometimes solitary (as in the gentians).

Plate 83.

AUSTRAL GENTIAN — *Gentianella diemensis*

The dainty Austral Gentian occurs in high places on the Australian mainland and Tasmania. It is common on the slopes of Mount Kosciusko (where the ones pictured were photographed) appearing in spring after the snows melt and remaining in bloom throughout the summer. Crocus-like flowers are white, lightly veined with mauve. Calyx and corolla are 5-lobed and the bright golden stamens are 5 in number. *G. diemensis* is an annual, and grows in quite large clumps, 30 cm or so high. Leaves are opposite, the lower ones oval and 2–3 cm or more long, the upper ones smaller and narrower.

FAMILY APIACEAE
(formerly Umbelliferae)

This family includes many food plants — carrots, parsnips, celery and culinary herbs and spices such as parsley, carraway, aniseed, and dill. Fennel and poison hemlock are also members. It is most prominent in the northern hemisphere, but is represented in most other parts of the world. Flowers in this family are carried in umbels, radiating like the ribs of an umbrella from the apex of a common stem.

Australian genera include *Aciphylla, Trachymene, Eryngium*, and *Xanthosia. Aciphylla glacialis* is the prickly-leafed, aromatic Alpine Celery, which grows above the tree-line in the Australian Alps, and bears sweetly scented, lacy white flowers. *Trachymene caerulea* is the dainty Blue Lace Flower of coastal limestone country around Perth, Western Australia. *Eryngium* species are the Sea Hollies. *Xanthosia* includes the 4-rayed Southern Cross (*Xanthosia rotundifolia*).

Plate 84.

FLANNEL FLOWERS — *Actinotus helianthi*

A. helianthi grows in rocky and sandy areas of coastal New South Wales and Queensland, sometimes occurring in great fields in the most arid and exposed situations, and blooming profusely in spring and summer.

Daisy-like, softly furred flowers, up to 8 cm across, consist of numerous green-tipped velvety white petal-like bracts, surrounding a dense cluster of individual flowers. The entire plant — flowers, buds, stems, and grey-green much-divided foliage — is covered with soft silky down, making the common name, Flannel Flower, most appropriate.

With the exception of one species which extends to New Zealand, *Actinotus* is an exclusively Australian genus, with main centres of development in coastal New South Wales and the south-west of Western Australia.

FAMILY CAMPANULACEAE
THE BLUEBELLS

The family Campanulaceae includes many garden favourites, the majority of them blue-flowered. It derives its name from the genus *Campanula* (Latin: little bell) — the genus which includes the bluebells of Scotland, the English harebells, and garden plants such as Canterbury bells. Its members are herbs (rarely shrubs) and are found mainly in the northern hemisphere, the majority in the Mediterranean region. The sole Australian representative is the widespread genus, *Wahlenbergia*.

Members of this family are herbaceous plants or undershrubs with milky juice. Leaves are nearly always alternate (rarely opposite); flowers are usually solitary. Fruit is a capsule.

Plate 85.

ALPINE BLUEBELL — *Wahlenbergia* species

In late summer, the high plateaux of the Australian Alps are bright with this dainty relative of the famous bluebells of Scotland. Nodding bell-like flowers, of varying shades of blue are borne singly on long stalks. Calyx and corolla are mostly 5-lobed, and there are 5 free stamens. Fruit is a capsule, containing numerous tiny seeds. *Wahlenbergia* is a mainly southern genus of the bluebell family, well represented in Australia and New Zealand, though South Africa is the main centre of development. Australian species are widely distributed in temperate regions. They are a complex group and the limits of some of the species are still under revision. The family Campanulaceae derives its name from the genus *Campanula* (Latin: little bell) — the genus which includes the Scottish bluebells, English harebells, and garden favourites such as Canterbury bells.

84

8

FAMILY GOODENIACEAE

THOUGH AUSTRALIA'S flora is predominantly endemic, insofar as individual species and even genera are concerned, in the main the major plant families of other continents are also the major plant families here. An exception is the Goodeniaceae, an almost entirely Australian family of over 300 species of herbs and undershrubs. Members are widespread throughout the continent, and major development is in the West: all the genera and over two-thirds of the species occur there. Only a handful of species extend beyond Australia, some occurring on various Pacific Islands and others ranging northward as far as South China.

Largest genus is *Goodenia*, with about 120 species, found in all States and the Northern Territory; all except one are confined to Australia. *Scaevola*, with over 70 species, is also found in all States; this genus includes strand plants of the sea coasts, and extends beyond Australia. There are 20 *Lechenaultia* species, all but three confined to Western Australia. *Dampiera* is a purely Australian genus of about 58 species, the majority Western Australian though some are found in all States and the Northern Territory.

Selliera is a genus of two species of creeping perennial herbs, one (*S. exigua*) endemic to Western Australia, the other (*S. radicans*) occurring in eastern States (except Queensland) and extending to New Zealand. This species has white flowers and spoon-shaped, succulent leaves. Fruit is a berry. It grows on the margins of salt marshes or along tidal streams. *Velleia* is a genus of about 20 species, found in both eastern and western States. Flowers are almost always yellow, an exception being the western species, *V. rosea*.

Flowers of the Goodeniaceae usually have 5 sepals and a 5-lobed, tubular corolla, usually split on one side, often giving the flowers the appearance of a spreading hand. There are 5 stamens, free or with anthers united in a ring around the style. A feature of the family is the unusual method of pollination. Stamens usually ripen while the flower is in bud. The style is long and broadens at the apex to form a cup (known botanically as indusium) usually fringed with hairs. As the style grows upwards the fringing hairs brush pollen from the anthers and collect it in the cup. At this stage the stigma is immature and hidden within the indusium; the flower is still in bud. When the flower opens the pollen either remains in the indusium or is forced by the growth of the stigma onto a brush of hairs or cuplike receptacles on the upper petals.

Plate 86.

BLUE LECHENAULTIA — *Lechenaultia biloba*

It is said the Pingarra Aborigines called this lechenaultia "the floor of the sky" — surely a most appropriate name for these flowers of almost unbelievably vivid blue, borne profusely from early winter to late summer. *L. biloba* is a low, spreading shrub, rarely more than 50 cm high, which grows naturally in gravel and sandy soils of southern and central Western Australia. Leaves are crowded, narrow and heathlike.

86

Plate 87.

RED LECHENAULTIA — *Lechenaultia formosa*

The flame-coloured flowers of the Red Lechenaultia are carried over a long period, but bloom most abundantly in spring. Leaves are short, narrow and crowded, and the plant is usually prostrate and matlike in habit. It is a native of the sand-plains of southern Western Australia.

Plate 88.

BLUE DAMPIERA — *Dampiera stricta*

This is an eastern Dampiera, occurring from Queensland to Tasmania, mainly on sandy soils. Branches are angular, and the stiff little leaves are sometimes toothed. It is a low shrub, with numerous erect stems. Bright blue, 5-petalled flowers are clothed in short, rusty hairs and are borne from early winter to mid-summer.

The genus *Dampiera* commemorates William Dampier, who collected the first specimens when he visited the north-west coast of Australia in 1698. It is an exclusively Australian genus, most of the 50-odd species being confined to the West. A distinguishing feature is that the lower edges of the upper petals fold inwards, forming little ear-shaped receptacles (auricles) which collect and hold the ripe pollen.

Plate 89.

RED AND YELLOW LECHENAULTIA — *Lechenaultia longiloba*

This lechenaultia is a prostrate shrub of the sandy heathlands around Geraldton, Western Australia. It flowers profusely in spring, carpeting the ground with vivid colour.

Plate 90.

PURPLE FAN-FLOWER — *Scaevola ramosissima*

The 5 winged petals of *Scaevola* species are arranged in a one-sided manner, rather like an opened fan or a hand with 5 outspread fingers. Corolla lobes are clothed with hairs, which collect pollen spilled from the indusium. *Scaevola ramosissima* is a native of eastern New South Wales, a scrambling plant with hairy stems, sparse, stalkless, narrow leaves, and large purple flowers. It occurs in heathlands and dry sclerophyll forests, and blooms for most of the year. *Scaevola calendulacea*, another eastern species, forms carpets on coastal sand-dunes; flowers and berries are bright blue. The pale-coloured *Scaevola hookeri* is a creeping prostrate mat-plant of mountainous regions.

87

88

89

90

FAMILY ASTERACEAE
(formerly Compositae)
THE DAISIES

THE DAISY family is the largest family of flowering plants in the world, and also the most widespread. There are probably 1,000 genera and over 20,000 species; they are found in all quarters of the globe, in habitats ranging from alpine to desert. Members are mainly herbs, though climbers, shrubs, and even trees occur. Included within this family are ornamentals such as dahlias, zinnias, asters, chrysanthemums, marigolds, and cornflowers, as well as the traditional daisies; weeds such as dandelions, cobbler's pegs, and Bathurst burrs; plants of economic importance — the chicory of commerce, vegetables such as lettuce and artichoke, sunflower, the seeds of which yield edible oil, and pyrethrum, source of an insect repellant. Numerically the family is the third largest in Australia, exceeded only by the Myrtaceae and the Proteaceae. There are probably at least 800 indigenous species, representing about 100 genera.

Flowers of the Daisy family are clustered into heads, attached to a common base and surrounded by one or several rows of bracts which perform the function of sepals, protecting the composite inflorescence in bud. In the individual flowers, sepals are replaced by hairs, bristles or scales (known botanically as pappus) or are absent. There are 5 petals, united into a corolla but showing their origin in 5 lobes or teeth. Sometimes the corolla is tubular, with 5 regular lobes, and sometimes it is ligulate, i.e. with the upper part extended in a tongue-like, toothed strap.

Members of the family can be divided into broad groups according to the structure of the flowers: sometimes the flowerhead consists entirely of tubular florets, as in *Craspedia* species (Billy Buttons, plate 93); sometimes all ligulate, as in dandelions. More often, as in the familiar daisy, there is a central disc of tubular flowers (called disc florets) surrounded by a ray of petal-like ligulate flowers (called ray florets). In these mixed types the disc florets are usually bisexual, while the ray florets are female or neuter — their main function, like that of petals in flowers of other families, being to attract pollinating insects.

The Asteraceae are among the most efficient of all flowering plants — this is why they are so widespread. Most are insect-pollinated, and as the conspicuous heads which attract these visitors each consist of many flowers, a single insect may fertilise many at a time. The perfect (bisexual) flowers have stamens (5 in number) with anthers united into a tube around the style. This style, with its immature

continues on page 94

Plate 91.

EVERLASTING SUNRAY — *Helipterum floribundum*

This member of the Asteraceae (Daisy family) is a desert plant — an annual herb of arid places — which blooms profusely after the seasonal rains, carpeting the barren plains with bright-eyed flowers. It is photographed here blooming at Alice Springs.

Helipterum is a genus of about 90 species of herbs or, rarely, shrubs. About 60 species are confined to Australia; the remainder are endemic to South Africa. *H. floribundum* is a low-growing ephemeral found in drier regions of all mainland States. The inflorescence consists of a central disk of bright yellow tubular florets, surrounded by several rows of snow-white, papery bracts.

91

stigmas, gradually lengthens, carrying the pollen out of the anther tube. Finally the stigmas spread, and expose their receptive inner surface, hitherto hidden. In effect, the flower is first male, then female, thus favouring cross-pollination rather than self-pollination. However, should cross-pollination be not effected, in many cases the stigmas finally curl back to receive pollen grains from the style below, thus ensuring self-pollination as a last resort.

Devices for the distribution of seeds are also varied and most efficient. Frequently, as in dandelions, the pappus (modified sepals) is hairy or silky, so that the whole structure acts like a parachute, enabling the fruit to be carried by the wind. In other cases, the pappus consists of stiff, barbed bristles, which cling to passing animals (the common weed, cobbler's peg, is an example).

Another device which has assisted the Asteraceae to become the largest family in the botanic world is the rosette of flat, radical leaves formed at the base of plants of many species — commandeering surrounding soil and depriving competitors of sunlight (though not each other, as the lower leaves in the rosette have longer stalks than those above them, so that each has its share of sunlight). Survival and propagation are also assisted by the roots, often thickened and sometimes tuberous, as in *Dahlia*. The "yam" of the Aborigines is an Australian example; its tuberous roots were sought for food.

Australia genera include desert and alpine "everlastings" such as *Helichrysum* (paper daisies) and *Helipterum* (sunrays) — flowers with papery involucral bracts often radiating beyond the composite head in a petal-like fashion; traditional daisylike plants such as *Brachycome, Senecio, Olearia*; and genera such as *Myriocephalus* and *continues on page* 98

Plate 92.

POACHED EGG DAISIES — *Myriocephalus stuartii*

The Poached Egg Daisies are desert ephemerals, sturdy plants up to 60 cm high which spring up in the dry interior after the wet season. Foliage is grey-green and woolly, with leaves narrow, alternate and entire. The erect stems are simple or branching only at the base. As with all members of the family, these spectacular daisies are composed of numerous tiny florets grouped into a composite head, but in this case the large flat compound head consists not just of crowded individual flowers but of numerous small branched floral heads, each consisting of a number of tiny tubular florets. These flowers are yellow, and form the "yolk" of the "poached egg"; the "white" consists of many rows of narrow bracts, surrounding the compound inflorescence. *Myriocephalus* is a purely Australian genus of 10 species. The specimen shown here and on the frontispiece was photographed blooming near Alice Springs, Northern Territory, in September.

Plate 93.

BILLY BUTTONS — *Craspedia uniflora*

This is a mountain daisy, found in temperate areas of all States, and extending also to New Zealand. In summertime it blooms profusely on the highlands of the Australian Alps; the specimen pictured was photographed near the summit of Mount Kosciusko. *C. uniflora* is an annual or perennial herb, which grows in little tufted clumps up to 50 cm high. Leaves are usually woolly, but it is a very variable plant and in some cases they are smooth. The little buttonlike compound flowerheads, about 2–3 cm across, vary in colour from almost white to deep orange — generally speaking the higher the altitude, the brighter the colour of the flowers. *Craspedia* is a genus of 4 species, all confined to Australia except the species pictured, which extends to New Zealand.

94

92

93

Plate 94.

PURPLE DAISY — *Brachycome* species

The purple-flowered *Brachycome* species pictured here was photographed flowering in September on remote Peron Peninsula, Western Australia. *Brachycome* is a mainly Australian genus of about 60 species of small herbaceous plants. They are to be found in all States and the Northern Territory, growing under conditions varying from near-desert to alpine. Leaves often form rosettes, and the solitary flowerheads are borne on long stems. The flowers are very like those of the English daisy and indeed the two genera are closely allied. The petal-like ray florets are white, yellow, pink, mauve, blue, or purple, according to species, and disc florets are yellow.

Plate 96.

GROUNDSEL — *Senecio* species

Senecio is the largest genus in the family Asteraceae: there are more than 1,300 species, ranging over nearly all the world. The generic name (from the Latin, *senex*, an old man) refers to the white beard-like pappus on the fruit. There are about 40 Australian species, all yellow-flowered, occurring in all States and the Northern Territory. The specimen pictured was photographed blooming at Alice Springs.

Plate 95.

DAISY BUSH — *Olearia tomentosa* (syn. *O. dentata*)

Olearia tomentosa is a small shrub, up to 2 m high, a native of eastern New South Wales and Victoria, sometimes growing on rocky seacoasts (the specimen pictured was photographed at North Head, Port Jackson). Leaves are large, dark green, and hairy, particularly on the upper surface, sometimes toothed and rough to the touch. The large flowerheads, up to 5 cm across, are usually white but may be blue or pinkish-mauve. *Olearia* is a mainly Australian genus of shrubs and undershrubs (rarely small trees), closely allied to the old world *Aster*. There are about 80 indigenous species, widely distributed throughout the continent. Most of the remaining species are confined to New Zealand, and a few occur in the highlands of New Guinea. The Musk Tree (*Olearia argophylla*) is an eastern Australian species which grows into a small tree 6 m or so high. Foliage and timber are fragrant.

Plate 97.

ALPINE DAISY — *Brachycome scapigera*

These are snow country daisies, one of several *Brachycome* species which bloom in the high country after the winter snows have melted. They grow in dense clumps, rising on slender stalks from a tuft of long, narrow, straplike leaves.

94

95

96

97

Craspedia, where the inflorescence consists of a number of small heads of tubular flowers, grouped together into a button-like dome or large flat disk.

Helichrysum is a genus of about 300 species of herbs and shrubs, well-distributed throughout the world. South Africa is the main centre of development, and Australia has about 100 species, all endemic. *Helichrysum* species are commonly known as paper daises, everlastings, or immortelles, and many, including the Australian species pictured, are cultivated as garden plants. Involucral bracts, often brightly coloured, are petaloid, stiff and papery, and usually extend beyond the composite head of tubular florets. In many species, such as the one pictured (plate 98), bracts are yellow, but in other species they may be white, pink, purple or brown. The florets are mostly yellow, and the floral heads may be small or large (in some species 5 cm or more in diameter). Leaves are alternate and entire, and foliage is often clothed in cottony wool.

Calotis is a purely Australian genus of 23 species. Dry-country herbs with representatives in all States except Tasmania, they are commonly called "burr daisies" because of the burr-like pappus of short, barbed bristles. Flowerheads are daisy-like, and the florets are usually coloured white, yellow or blue, occasionally mauve or pink.

Australian relatives of the European edelweiss belong to the closely allied genus, *Ewartia*. There are 4 indigenous species, all found in alpine areas of Tasmania, though one, *E. nubigena,* extends to the mainland and is found in the higher, exposed and stony places of the Australian Alps, on the slopes of Mount Bogong and Mount Kosciusko, forming compact, cushion-like plants with silvery grey foliage and bearing masses of tiny, stalkless flowerheads, brownish in colour and surrounded by white to pinkish bracts.

Plate 98.

GOLDEN PAPER DAISY or SUNGOLD —
Helichrysum bracteatum

The generic name *Helichrysum*, from the Greek *helios*, the sun, and *khrysos*, gold, suggests the appropriate alternative common name, Sungold, for these shining paper daisies. They are found in all States and the Northern Territory, growing in profusion on inland plains after seasonal rain and highland plateaux after the snows melt, carpeting vast areas with burnished gold. *H. bracteatum* is an erect perennial, ranging in height from a few centimetres to over a metre. Flowerheads are large, sometimes up to 5 cm across. Foliage is aromatic; the upper leaves are long and narrow, and the lower ones heart-shaped and stem-clasping.

FAMILY LILIACEAE

THE LILIES

THE LILY family is a large one, widespread throughout the world, mainly in warm and temperate regions. It includes garden ornamentals such as tulips and hyacinths, vegetables such as the onion group, and asparagus. Members are herbs or occasionally shrubby climbers, usually with bulbs, rhizomes, corms, or with fibrous roots thickened into tubers. Leaves are linear and grasslike, with parallel veins; often they grow in a tuft from the base of the plant. Flowers of the Liliaceae have a calyx of three sepals and a corolla of three petals. Usually the sepals are petaloid, and in many cases they are almost indistinguishable from the petals. There are usually 6 stamens, and the style is often 3-lobed. The ovary (seedbox) is superior, that is, situated above the base of the petals and sepals. Fruit is a capsule or a berry.

Australia has no true lilies (*Lilium* species) but the family is represented by over 30 other genera, including *Blandfordia*, the Christmas Bells of eastern Australia, *Thysanotus*, the Fringe Lilies, *Burchardia* (Milkmaids), *Dianella* (Blueberry or Flax Lilies), *Calectasia* (Tinsel Lilies), *Sowerbaea* (Vanilla Lilies), and *Anguillaria* (Early Nancy).

Dianella is a genus of about 20 species, found in Australia, New Zealand and South America, and extending to Indonesia and south-east Asia. Flowers are blue, nodding, and carried in loose sprays; fruit is a colourful blue berry. Leaves are mostly basal. The genus *Bulbine* is mainly South African, but there are two endemic species, widespread in all Australian States and the Northern Territory. *Bulbine* species have soft leaves and usually have bulbous roots. *Stypandra* species are found in all States. They are tufted,

continues on page 102

Plate 99.

CHRISTMAS BELLS — *Blandfordia nobilis*

These dainty, red and yellow, bell-like flowers once grew profusely in damp places in the sandstone country around Sydney, dotting the open heathlands with colour at Christmas-time, the stiff, waxy little bells dancing and chattering with each passing breeze. They are becoming rarer with suburban development but can still be seen growing naturally in the extensive national parks on the city's outskirts — Kuring-gai Chase to the north, and Royal National Park to the south. The Hawkesbury sandstone country is a treasure-house of native plants — over 2000 different species have already been described, more than the total number of species in the whole of the British Isles. Many are endemic, occurring nowhere else in the world, and their continued survival in what is now the most densely populated area of Australia depends largely on the existence of national parks such as those mentioned above.

B. nobilis, a member of the Lily family, has no bulb but a thickened root-stock. Rigid, slender, grasslike leaves spring from the base of the plant, crowded around the slender, erect flower-stems with their racemes of waxy bells. The floral tube consists of 3 petaloid sepals and 3 petals, fused together to form a 6-lobed bell. There are 6 stamens, fused to the perianth tube for half the distance. Fruit is a long, triangular capsule. This species is confined to New South Wales, and occurs mainly in the Hawkesbury sandstone country.

Blandfordia is a genus of 4 species, all endemic to eastern Australia. *B. cunninghamii* with flowers larger and deeper in colour than those of *B. nobilis* and with more strap-shaped leaves, is a mountain species, confined to New South Wales and occurring on peaty soil in the Blue Mountains; *B. grandiflora* is similar to *B. nobilis* but has larger flowers and extends from the Hawkesbury River into northern New South Wales and Queensland; *B. marginata* is confined to Tasmania, where it is commonly called the Gordon River Lily.

grasslike herbs with fibrous roots; flowers are usually blue (rarely white) and carried in loose sprays; they resemble those of *Dianella*.

Calectasia is a monotypic genus now classified by some botanists into a separate family. The single species is *C. cyanea*, the Blue Tinsel Lily, a small, wiry shrub with stiff, crowded, heathlike leaves. Starlike, papery flowers are solitary at the ends of short branchlets. Petals and petaloid sepals are lustrous deep blue or purple, and anthers are bright gold. Its main development is on the sand plains of south Western Australia, but it extends to South Australia and western Victoria.

There are a number of other native species which are commonly called "lilies" but actually belong to other families — for example, the Gymea Lily, *Doryanthes excelsa*, which is a member of the related family, Agavaceae, and the Rock Lily, *Dendrobium speciosum*, which is an orchid. Conversely, genera which until recently were regarded as belonging to the Lily family include such un-lilylike plants as *Xanthorrhoea*, the Grasstree or Blackboy, *Eustrephus*, the climbing, orange-berried Wombat Berry, *Ripogonum*, the Lawyer Vine of eastern rainforests, and *Smilax* the Native Sarsaparilla.

Plate 100.

FRINGE-LILY — *Thysanotus tuberosus*

This Fringe Lily is a native of eastern Australia, an erect, slender plant with long grasslike leaves and delicately fringed violet flowers, carried on long, smooth stems. Roots are tuberous, and fruit is a round capsule. It flowers in spring and summer, and is common in grassy heathlands of the sandstone country. Three broad fringed petals and 3 narrow shining sepals form the perianth. With the exception of one species which extends to South China and the Philippines, *Thysanotus* is a wholly Australian genus of the Lily family. There are about 30 species; one or more occurs in every State, but the richest development is in Western Australia, where 27 species have been described.

Plate 101.

VANILLA LILY — *Sowerbaea juncea*

The common name, Vanilla Lily, refers to the delicate perfume of these dainty little pink or lilac flowers. They are borne at the end of long slender stalks, in crowded clusters surrounded by papery bracts. Individual flowers open one or two at a time, so that the clusters consist mainly of unopened buds and the colourful, persistent sepals and petals of flowers that have closed, highlighted by an odd, wide-eyed bloom. *S. juncea* is an eastern species, commonly found in damp, almost swampy places. It is a little tufted rushlike plant (an alternative common name is Rush-lily). The long narrow leaves are soft and fleshy, rather like those of the onion group. Roots are fibrous, and the plant, spreading by short underground stems, often forms large clumps in open, grassy situations. *Sowerbaea* is a wholly Australian genus of 3 species, the other 2 species being confined to the West.

Plate 102.

MILKMAIDS — *Burchardia umbellata*

Wide-open, starlike, creamy white flowers, sometimes delicately tinged with pink, carried at the end of slender, unbranched stems 30 cm or more long, make this common plant of sandy places a dainty addition to the floral scene in spring and summer. There are 3 petals and 3 petal-like sepals, almost identical in appearance. The 6 stamens, tipped with purple anthers, emphasise the creamy whiteness of the flowers. Leaves are soft and stem-clasping; roots are fibrous. *B. umbellata* is confined to Australia, and is widespread throughout all States. The only other species in the genus, *B. multiflora*, is restricted to the west.

100

102

FAMILY PHILESIACEAE

Plate 103.

WOMBAT BERRY or BLACKFELLOW'S ORANGES — *Eustrephus latifolius*

E. latifolius is a much-branched, wiry-stemmed leafy climber which grows in damp situations on the eastern Australian coast and mountains, scrambling sometimes several metres over shrubs and trees. Leaves are large, glossy, and parallel-veined. Small fringed flowers, white, pale pink, or mauve, are borne in spring, clustered in the axils of the upper leaves. The fruit, a bright orange berry about a centimetre across, is carried in summer and autumn. *E. latifolius* is endemic to eastern Australia. It produces small edible tubers, which Aborigines sought for food.

The genus was formerly included in the family Liliaceae: flowers have 3 sepals, 3 petals, 6 stamens and a superior ovary.

FAMILY IRIDACEAE

The family Iridaceae, includes well known garden plants such as iris, freesia, gladiolus and crocus. It is a widespread family, found in most parts of the world but most abundantly in South Africa and tropical America. Members are herbs, with corms, tuberous roots or rhizomes. They differ from members of the closely allied family Liliaceae in that the ovary (seedbox) is inferior — that is, situated below the petals and sepals — and stamens are 3 in number (in Liliaceae there are 6 stamens). There are 5 Australian genera, the largest being *Patersonia*. The monotypic genus *Hewardia* is confined to Tasmania, the single species being *H. tasmanica*, the mountain iris.

Plate 104.

PURPLE FLAG-LILY or BUSH IRIS — *Patersonia sericea*

This native iris is the bright herald of spring in the sandstone country of eastern Australia. Its flamboyant purple flags appear early in the season, heading the profusion of gay flowers which later carpet the heathlands. They are will-o'-the-wisps which appear in profusion, then disappear, only to appear again within a few hours, as bountifully as before. The reason for this tantalising behaviour is that each individual flower blooms only a few short hours, opening in the morning and quickly fading in the heat of the noon sun. But each flower is only one of several, tightly packed within the same sheathing bracts. It is quickly replaced by another opening bud, so that to the casual glance it appears as though the withered flower of yesterday has miraculously renewed itself.

Patersonia is a genus of about 20 species, all Australian except 3 which extend northwards into New Guinea, Borneo, and the Philippines. The generic name commemorates William Paterson, Lieut.-Governor of New South Wales from 1800 to 1810, and an early botanical collector in Australia. They are perennial herbs with tough, grasslike leaves and underground rhizomes. Flowers are borne in terminal clusters surrounded by 2 large sheathing bracts, from which the flowers arise, one or two at a time, over a period. There are 3 sepals and 3 petals — the petals are small and inconspicuous; it is the delicate, spreading sepals that form the colourful "flags". Fruit is a narrow, triangular capsule, which bursts open when ripe, scattering the seeds.

103

104

FAMILY AGAVACEAE

Plate 105.

GYMEA LILY — *Doryanthes excelsa*

Aborigines of the Illawarra tribe called this flower "Gymea"; it is also commonly known as the Giant Spear Lily (the generic name, *Doryanthes*, from the Greek, means "spear-flower") and sometimes as Flame Lily or Illawarra Lily. Whatever the common name applied, *D. excelsa* is truly a spectacular plant. Red fleshy trumpet-shaped flowers, nearly up to 15 cm long, are borne in dense rounded heads as large as cabbages, on stalks 5 m or more high arising from a rosette of giant leaves, up to 2 m long. A native of eastern New South Wales and Queensland, it grows particularly profusely in the Hawkesbury sandstone country. In spring the traveller on the main coastal highways around Sydney is greeted by the sight of thousands of these giant flowers which in bushland areas line the roadside in majestic and almost continuous display.

Doryanthes is a genus of 2 species, both of which occur only on the east coast of Australia. Leaves are fibrous, and arise in tufts from short branching rhizomes. Flowers are borne in large terminal heads. There are 6 perianth segments (3 sepals and 3 petals) the lobes spreading open and curling over at the top but tightly packed together at the base to form a container the shape and size of a wineglass, filled to overflowing with nectar (birds are the visitors). Stamens, 6 in number, have large, conspicuous, pollen-laden anthers. Fruit is a woody 3-celled capsule which splits open when ripe to reveal rows of flat winged seeds, the size and shape of a ten-cent piece. *Doryanthes* was formerly included in the Amaryllidaceae (the Daffodil family), but is now often regarded as belonging to the Agavaceae. Both families are closely allied to the lilies, differing chiefly in the ovary, which is inferior.

FAMILY HAEMODORACEAE

Plate 106.

RED-AND-GREEN KANGAROO PAW — *Anigosanthos manglesii*

The quaint furry Kangaroo Paws are confined to Western Australia and the species pictured. *A. manglesii*, is the floral emblem of that State. It is common on the sandy coastal plains of the south-western province, growing in profusion in the bushland around the capital city, Perth. Flowers are borne in terminal racemes at the top of long woolly stems, often up to a metre high and almost as colourful as the flowers themselves, arising from a tuft of smooth, grasslike leaves. Calyx and corolla are fused to form a 6-lobed elongated tube which, as the flower opens, splits down one side; the tube then becomes flat and ribbonlike, and the perianth lobes roll back, revealing 6 stamens in orderly row.

Anigosanthos is a genus of lilylike herbs with long grasslike leaves springing in tufts from short rhizomes. There are 10 species, all confined to the south-west of Western Australia. Flowers and flower stems are clothed with numerous woolly hairs. *A. humilis*, the Catspaw, is a low-growing member of the group, with flowers varying in colour from gold to rusty red. *A. viridis* the Green Kangaroo Paw, has flowers of emerald green. The genus was until recently regarded as belonging to the worldwide family Amaryllidaceae, which includes jonquil, and snowdrop; it has now been reclassified into a separate family, Haemadoraceae.

105

106

FAMILY ORCHIDACEAE

THE ORCHIDS

ORCHIDS ARE commonly regarded as rare flowers, but actually they comprise one of the largest and most successful families of flowering plants in the world, rivalled only by the ubiquitous daisies (family Asteraceae). There are about 450 genera and probably 20,000 species — over 2,500 species have been described from New Guinea alone — and they are widespread throughout the world, though the epiphytic types are mainly tropical and subtropical in distribution.

Orchids are perennial herbs, usually with entire leaves alternate or radical, sometimes reduced to scales or almost absent. They vary in size from minute to large. Some are epiphytic, growing high on the branches of trees in jungle and rainforest, not parasitic but deriving their food supplies from air, sun, water, and decaying vegetable matter, often with creeping rhizomes and aerial roots or with stem thickened and bulblike; others are lithophytes, growing on bare rock. Many are terrestrial, growing in the ground and deriving nourishment through leaves and roots in the manner of most plants (most of these types form tubers). A few are saprophytes, plants with neither leaves nor green parts to transform the sun's energy into growth; they absorb their nutrients, with the help of certain fungi, from dead and decaying organic matter in the ground (the Australian Hyacinth Orchid, *Dipodium punctatum*, is an example).

Australia is well endowed with orchids; there are over 600 species, ranging from the spectacular Swamp Orchid (*Phaius tankervilliae*) with flowers 10 cm across, to the microscopic *Bulbophyllum minutissimum*, smallest orchid in the world: its flowers are almost too small to see, but tiny pseudo-bulbs reflect light so that the plant gleams and glistens in the sun like a jewel-box. Many of Australia's orchids are sweetly perfumed, some are unique in structure, strange and interesting in form.

Plate 107.

COOKTOWN ORCHID — *Dendrobium bigibbum*

Official floral emblem for the State of Queensland, this epiphytic orchid has dark pink flowers, often 5 cm or more across, carried profusely on long sprays. It grows on branches of trees in elevated areas of northern Queensland.

Plate 108.

ROCK LILY — *Dendrobium speciosum*

This Australian orchid has many variations in colour and form. The fragrant flowers, often quite small but sometimes almost 5 cm across, may be golden, creamy or pure white. The form pictured here, found in the Hawkesbury sandstone area, is a rock-dweller; the variety *D. speciosum* var. *hillii*, commonly called King Orchid, is found almost exclusively on trees, sometimes on branches more than 30 m up in the air, forming huge clumps with racemes sometimes containing hundreds of individual blooms. *Dendrobium* is a genus which extends beyond Australia, and there are a number of widely cultivated exotic species and hybrids. The endemic species are confined to coastal and mountain areas, from Tasmania to northern Australia.

Plate 109.

SPOTTED SUN ORCHID — *Thelymitra ixioides*

The Spotted Sun Orchid is a terrestrial, found in all States and New Zealand. Unlike most orchids, the labellum (lip) is very little different from the other petals. Bright blue (rarely pink) flowers are carried in racemes on slender stems sometimes up to 60 cm high. They open fully only in bright sunlight.

107

108

109

INDEX

Light figures indicate text page references.
Bold figures indicate colour plate numbers.